THE FULL CLEVELAND

A Novel

Terry Reed

Simon & Schuster

New York London Toronto Sydney

SIMON & SCHUSTER
Rockefeller Center
1230 Avenue of the Americas
New York, NY 10020

SIMON & SCHUSTER and colophon are registered trademarks
of Simon & Schuster, Inc.

For information about special discounts for bulk purchases,
please contact Simon & Schuster Special Sales:
1-800-456-6798 or business@simonandschuster.com

Book design by Ellen R. Sasahara

Manufactured in the United States of America

10   9   8   7   6   5   4   3   2   1

Library of Congress Cataloging-in-Publication Data
Reed, Terry, date.
 The full Cleveland / Terry Reed.
  p. cm.
 I. Title.
PS3618.E43585F85 2004
813'.6—dc22   2004052529

ISBN 0-7432-6273-5

To my parents
And their children
And their children

Acknowledgments

You know who you are to me and you know what you did: Terry McDonell, David Rosenthal, Denise Roy, Christina Richardson, David Kuhn, Leigh Feldman, Richard Giser, Kirsten Dehner, Fred Botwinik, John Homans, Angela Britzman, Jane Clark, Peter Wilkinson, Peter Kreutzer, Elizabeth Royte, Jon Glascoe, Joe Pierson, Nancy Butkus, David Auchincloss, Sheryl Lukomski, Sarah Jewler, Philippe Qualisse, Deborah Zdobinski, Jeff Ballsmeyer, Kay Arav, Paul Scott Drake, David Colbert, Jan Van Laere, Jack Barth, Ilene Schneiderman, Christa Worthington, Christopher Horn, Mark Reed, Sally Reed, Leslie Reed, Michael Neubarth, Ike Reed, Zarifah Reed, Lisa Reed, and John Seabrook. Thank you.

THE FULL CLEVELAND

TEN

When we were rich, we had no real use for the Easter Bunny.

We had an Egg Man. When I found out other children had the Bunny, I didn't envy them. Because either way it's your father, of course, and a father is an important thing and things happen to them over time, plus I'd just rather not have the Easter Bunny. Who needs the embarrassment. Especially if you went downtown and found him in Public Square trying to amuse everyone as well as sell them something, except he was eight feet tall and his eyes didn't blink and his teeth didn't move and some of the smaller children started screaming or sobbing and had to be instantly whisked into the arms of their mothers. All because of the Easter Bunny. No, I'm sorry, I mean maybe I should apologize, but we had Egg Man.

But I already said, that's when we were rich.

Easter Sunday, Egg Man was in charge of hiding. He was very good at it, so it was natural to think it came to him naturally. He hid chocolate eggs in baskets from us and jewelry and such in a blue box from Mother, but the main thing is, he did it with clues, and the whole thing got harder as you got older. We had a big house, and Egg Man made sure finding the stuff was almost impossible.

Mother said it was so Protestant of him. To maybe make us

look until Christmas. Once Mother had to, her clues were so hard.

Egg Man hid other things also from Mother. Easter afternoon, after she took us to church, he took over and took us to Cleveland. To the worst parts of it, was the best part. Which was the part he hid from Mother. It was about the one thing he did alone with us all year, but it was a good one. Sometimes it was to a river he claimed was famous for burning. The Cuyahoga, it was called, but Matt called it The Combustible. It had already caught fire twice, see, so Matt said that was the name for it.

Easter when I was still ten, all of the hidden things had been found except Mother's.

Noon mass was over and Clarine, Matt, Cabot, Luke, Lucy, and I were all packed in Mother's blue Buick convertible, except the top wasn't down. It was hot but we were helpless, because Mother was hanging back in the church parking lot, planning to talk to people. That's what she did after church on Sunday and it was much worse on Easter. We were usually used to it, but today we wanted to get home and see about Egg Man.

But a woman in a wide black hat saw Mother across the parking lot and started over on her walker. All of us in the hot car moaned. Clarine flashed dark eyes around, so we stopped. Then she told us to roll our windows all the way down.

Clarine was the oldest except for our parents. She lived with us and all, but she wasn't our sister. She was really the nanny, but really the housekeeper. Today she sat up where Mother would sit if Egg Man were driving. Shotgun, Matt liked to make a big point of calling it.

Like Egg Man himself, Clarine wasn't Catholic. Today she'd come to see the Easter hats, to hold Lucy, and maybe for curiosity, because in Catholic Church, you can see people kneel down. During mass, she hadn't knelt down herself, though. When I'd tried to not do it with her, Mother had frowned.

"Boyce, girl," Clarine had whispered when I tried it. "Do like the others." But at first I thought she said, Do *unto* others. It was an unbelievable coincidence, to have that happen in church, and instead of praying like I was supposed to, I sat around smiling about it.

Matt was the oldest. He sat up front, his head all slumped, due to staring down chronically at his new double-breasted, brass-buttoned blazer. He'd complained that morning that cool kids would see it. Now he lifted his head for about the first time since being ordered into the jacket regardless. "People," he said, "let us pray. Let us pray she doesn't run into any more people." He said it with his hands up, palms out, as if he had self-appointed himself our personal preacher. It was pretty funny, but you couldn't laugh too much or he'd do a ton more of it.

Clarine said, "Children. Please. Shut up." Which was something, because she usually said, "Children, please hush up." She was from the South, and that's where they say that. But "shut up" wasn't even allowed. Even for adults, strictly forbidden.

But she sure had said it, and Cabot and I turned to look at each other, bumping our hats with the streamers. We were so close in age, we had to wear the same hats. Except Cabot had long blond hair and looked like a picture from a magazine that sometimes features the world's most presentable children. Pictured in a riding habit with a horse, I bet, riding along with her beautiful mother. That *Town and Country*, no doubt. Anyway, under my hat, I had a crew cut.

Luke, in pint-size brown loafers, sat with his legs and arms ramrod straight and his eyes squeezed shut, bearing up under the delay rather nicely. He'd once had special preschool psychologists who had taught him to do that.

Over Clarine's shoulder, Lucy tried to wing her own head off, but then I suppose she gave up. Her Easter bonnet went all cock-eyed, and she had to peer around the brim of it to still see us in back. This made her appear of debatable character for a two-year-old, like one of those questionable men in the movies you're not allowed to watch, the ones with the guns and the crooked fedoras.

I knew in my heart church hadn't made any difference.

We had been quite in love with each other inside when we were told to thank God and sing Hallelujah, but now we'd forgotten all that, because of Mother keeping us waiting. If we didn't get home soon Easter was pointless. Egg Man might say it was too late for Cleveland.

During the sermon, my stomach felt strange, though to be fair to the speaker that could have been chocolate for breakfast. But it did seem that every time you tried to really listen to a preacher, you automatically heard about another leper. Then I decided it wasn't chocolate or lepers. The problem was, I was lapsing. Which can happen to Catholics. Lapsing made my stomach feel strange, is all that I'm saying.

Outside the Buick, Mother was still stalling.

Mrs. Taft waddled over, trailed by two more ladies with canes and heavy pearl necklaces. They all stared wide-eyed into the Buick and Mother introduced us for the first time since last Sunday. We said, How do you do, smiled and everything and possibly would have curtsied if we could have, and then we resented those poor ladies for it. Even if Egg Man weren't Protestant, this was the part of church he wouldn't be going for.

The ladies straightened up so we could see only the pearls and eyeglasses tangled hopelessly at their stomachs. Then they told Mother how weren't we simply the sweetest-looking family, with simply the handsomest children with simply the biggest blue eyes and simply the cutest blue coats and simply the longest blond hair. Except the windows were open and we could hear all of it.

In whispers, we complained about the factual errors they'd made. Such as Matt's hair was almost black, almost like Mother's. And mine wasn't long and blond because of the crew cut. I told the others maybe their code word was *simply,* and they were telling each other in code we were a *simple* family, see, as in not so smart, without having to break the bad news to Mother.

At that, Clarine looked displeased, then changed her mind and chuckled, but with a certain finality. Amen, is what she was saying. Could make you suspicious *she* thought we were simple. But all she actually said was, "Boyce, girl, now hush up now." She said it the usual way, nice and soft and southern. With a smile, even.

Then the last car in the lot pulled out. But Mother must have been hoping for one last slowpoke in a wheelchair, because now she began fishing around in her purse finding her keys and inching around the car to check the door was closed okay for the baby. When two more ladies popped up in the windshield, we all groaned without even trying to muffle it. "Hush up. Now." This time she wasn't smiling.

The longer we waited in enforced silence, the more I was forced to think about church.

After the sermon, Father Dietz had asked for the quiet necessary to search everybody's consciences. Except he said "social" consciences, I think in honor of people who didn't exactly live in the neighborhood. Since I didn't know where to find that one, how could I search it? I looked up at Mother.

But she was already searching. Her head was bowed and her eyes were closed and her lips were pursed. I wondered if having a social conscience made you beautiful, with smooth skin and a sweet mouth and good taste in clothing. Mother's made her look like a chic saint, one dressed up in a smart, navy blue wool suit. I tugged on her sleeve.

She opened one eye, put her finger to her mouth, shook her head frowning, and went back to searching. She was fed up, you could tell, because that was after the do unto others.

I suddenly felt sorry about the old ladies. So I looked around to my brothers and sisters and said maybe Mother was just out there acting Christian, to lonely people because it was Easter Sunday and all, and we should be nice and quiet about it.

Clarine nodded approval, and nobody said anything for a while. Then Matt said between acting Christian and glomming-up compliments about your sideshow kids, tell me the difference.

Clarine turned and glared at him.

Then Cabot said, "Hey, only the front seat's a sideshow."

And Matt mumbled, "The backseat's a bigger one." And he glanced at Clarine, like he was actually expecting backup, her being an official front-seater like himself.

And Cabot said, "Hey, Matt? What's with the blazer?"

And Luke finally exploded with, "But what about CLEVE-LAND?!"

And we *all* said hush up, because Mother couldn't know that's where Dad took us on Easters. She couldn't hear about Cleveland. It was downtown.

Then finally God sent Batman out to save us. Through the church doors here came Father Dietz all in black, flashing his pastor cape with a flourish, making a big thing of it, making us laugh, opening the car door and installing Mother in behind the wheel, as if even God had had enough of her loitering in his parking lot. We cried, "Bye, Father Dietz, thank you! Happy Easter! Thanks a million!" And then we were finally off, heading for home.

Except we forgot another tradition. On Easter and other Holy Days of Obligation, Mother sometimes celebrated after church by taking a spin around Shaker Heights, looking at everyone's houses. Even though Matt said, "Are you serious?" Mother automatically took the turn to start the tour at South Park Boulevard. Cabot and I crashed hats again turning to shake our heads at each other. Cleveland was becoming out of the question. Although secretly, we both liked this part of it, the looking at everyone's houses.

On the first corner was Matt's friend Rey McDowell's house. Frankly, it looked like the White House. It was painted-white sandstone, like the White House, and was about as wide as the White House, though not quite as tall. But the prettiest part wasn't even the house, it was the way it was wrapped like a present, with its rounded-off hedge, which rippled like a long green ribbon over the top of the hill, down the hill, around the corner, and across the front, ending in a nice pink bow of rhododendrons over where my friend Mickey Knight's flat-topped hedge began. That is, Mickey Knight's parents' flat-topped hedge.

That hedge grew so high you couldn't even see Mickey's house, but if you could, it was really quite pretty. As we went by, Cabot said, "Gee, looks like everyone's gone on vacation." Then they all started grumbling how come we didn't get to go, spring skiing or something, which started sounding so bratty, I was embarrassed to be with them.

I said, "Relax. Maybe we can't afford to."

Mother frowned at me in the rearview mirror.

"Well, we're not as rich as the McDowells, right?"

But it was as if Mother had you on remote control through her tiny mirror, though, because I instantly said, "Excuse me."

You weren't allowed to mention money, much less who was very rich and who wasn't. That and lying. Plus saying shut up and you guys. And of course telling people our house cost a dollar.

Mother's raised eyebrow was still in the mirror. "Boyce, honey? What's the matter? Don't you feel well?"

I didn't answer right off. I didn't know what the matter was anymore, or if there was even a word for it. But Mother's eye was still waiting. So under pressure like that, I chose a weird one. "Me? I'm remarkable."

Luke reached across Cabot and patted me sympathetically. He knew I wasn't *remarkable*. That was an old person's word. You'd have to be almost dead to come up with it.

I slid closer to my window and looked out, getting ready for my other best friend's house, Mickey Joslyn's. I'd always thought Mickey's was the best Tudor ever made, because it wasn't one of those tall, phony-looking Tudors, it was sort of low Tudor, old Tudor, hacked-up Tudor, as if a couple of Tudor warriors carved out a house there say five hundred years ago. About eight of the bedrooms had fireplaces big enough to cook a moose in, but my favorite room was Mickey's mother's. It was blue and yellow, which may not sound too good, but it was that certain blue, the color not really of the sea, but what the sea should be, and there were a couple of yellow things tossed around, say a pillow on the bed to break up the blue, or when you stepped into the room you'd probably start thinking you were walking on water. There was also a Monet painting on one of the walls, and it had a sea in it, exactly the color the sea should be.

I already said, I liked looking at everyone's houses.

•　•　•

Then it was extremely quiet in the car, because of Grandfather's house. Once you passed the second Mickey's, the next corner was Grandfather's, or at least Grandfather's house before he died. Everybody said, *There's Grandfather's*. It was definitely our favorite one.

It was just an old brick house with wings on either side, but we could remember being in there, and sinking back carefully into big, upholstered chairs with cake balanced on china plates, and being no taller than the dining room table itself, and it made you sit still in the car to think it all ended because Grandfather died. I didn't say it out loud because of not mentioning money, but when I saw his house, I remembered how he gave us ours for a dollar.

I was two, and we came to Grandmother's funeral from New York City, where Mother and Dad and Matt and Cabot and I lived then. After, there was a ride in a long line of cars with lights on at noon, then another ride, through these very streets, in Grandfather's old Mercury, a car he christened that day for our benefit, naming it the Dream Machine. And then our house, surrounded by flowers, filled up with furniture by Grandfather and long kept a secret from Grandmother (who could never really know because she could never really approve Dad's marrying a Catholic), and then Matt, Cabot, and me running all through and around, and then Dad and Grandfather shaking hands, and Dad opening his brown wallet and handing over one single green dollar. Looking at Grandfather's, I remembered now how I never forgot that.

"Hallelujah," Matt said, but not with his hands up. "It's over, you guys."

Mother said, "Matt."

We circled back to South Park and then to our house. Ours was nice and everything, but it didn't look like the Magic Kingdom like some of the others. It was just big and brick with a lot of windows.

In the sunlight, they were shiny and dark, and the panes in the French doors almost looked like so many mirrors, and in them you could see reflections so intricate you could practically watch the wind blowing in the trees. That was all there was to it.

Though of course the inside also, with Grandfather's touch on it. The tall front windows had been treated in pale silk curtains finished with a slash of valance at the top, the ornate moldings had been stripped of paint, the walls papered in the faintest eggshell. In the dining room, the original old murals depicting faint green hills and glowing stacks of hay and a shepherd boy in a gold straw hat tending round gray sheep had been restored as well as reasonable, then left to delicately crack and peel. The wood floors downstairs were covered with old rugs Grandfather probably rolled up and carted off from his own house when Grandmother wasn't looking. Then Grandfather had retiled the bathrooms, filled up the linen closets, and stuffed the library with books. In the basement, he fitted out a toolroom, a playroom, and a sort of a gym. You'd have to say, it had almost everything.

I looked up at Mother. She was already leaning forward a little, peering through the windshield as we rounded the curve in the driveway, looking, like all of us, to make sure Egg Man was there. When he strolled out of the shadows of the garage into the sunlight, we knew we were finally home.

The Buick stopped right up beside Dad. Mother rolled down her window and stuck her face out, her green eyes blinking up, her long dark hair falling back, looking pretty but also impertinent, like a belle, from the South, which she wasn't. She was born in New York City.

We all watched them kiss, though today's wasn't one of their best ones. Dad's weekend wardrobe was probably why, especially on Easter Sunday. His same old paint-splattered khaki pants, canvas shoes, and white oxford shirt with the rips up the sleeves. Today he had Grandfather's old gray felt hat also, pushed back a little which made him look like a boy, though a tall one. Mother liked him when he looked like an adman, in a proper suit and tie. That's what he wore to work, but the minute he came home, he changed into something sloppy. She tried to upgrade him, she bought him cashmere smoking jackets with satin collars and such, but he'd just say "ah" when he opened the box, and that was the last you'd see of it. Anyway, you could tell by the kiss, she sure wasn't backing down on the wardrobe thing, especially on Easter Sunday.

Dad put his hand on the top of the Buick, leaned down and looked in at us.

"Hi, Egg Man!" we all cried, making sure to call him that and not Dad today.

"Fair enough," he said. "My turn. Into the car." He swung around and went for the garage, and after Cabot and I nearly knocked off our hats grinning at each other, we climbed out of her blue Buick convertible and into his blue Buick hardtop. They really liked Buicks, is all I can tell you.

"Georgie boy," Mother said while Dad snapped Lucy into the car seat. That's what she called him when she wanted an answer, which was sometimes hard as anything to get out of him. "Just give me a hint. Just one little rhymed clue where you're all going."

Luke rolled down his window. "You're supposed to call him Egg Man."

Mother reached in and put her hand on Luke's head, so she could shut him up without having to come right out and say so. She smirked at Dad and said, "Egg Man? What's the itinerary?"

Dad got in the driver's seat and stroked his chin, taking his time, so we'd all know how tough it was to come up with this stuff. "Hmmm. I'm not winking . . ."

We already started to look around at one another.

". . . I'm *thinking*."

This was a hard one.

"I'm smart, and I'm art."

Mother frowned. "Not that statue at the Museum, George. Not *The Thinker*."

I said, "Art?" Are you kidding. I'd been planning all day to see a river that burns. "Hey, *Dad*?"

He turned and winked at me. "Hey, Zu," he said, which is an extra name he called me because of some movie.

"George, that statue was bombed. With dynamite."

It was? I didn't know that part.

Dad said, "Then how about some nice ducks in the pond?"

Only Luke looked anywhere close to bowled over.

"But the ducks are at the Museum, George. In the lagoon." You could tell, she didn't want us to run into *The Thinker*. Which only made us want to, to tell you the truth.

"Roses are red, boxes are blue," Dad said, rolling up his window and reminding Mother she had some finding to do. If she didn't find her blue box, she just didn't get it. She might get more rhymed clues, but not the blue box and the thing she always liked that was in it. I already said, he'd let her look for a year.

As we went down the driveway, we turned in our seats to see Mother and Clarine, waving. They were like those two faces on the velvet curtains when you went for children's plays at the Cleveland Playhouse. One laughing, one frowning. Clarine was laughing. But poor Mother, she hated losing us. To a Protestant, probably, and on a Holy Day of Obligation.

On the way to the ducks, we asked Dad more than once if he didn't have something slightly more spectacular in mind for after, something more like a river that burns. But he didn't answer. We just had to pray we'd see something worse.

We expected the ducks would be corny, but I guess we were wrong. Besides, Dad said it was a fine old tradition, for the people of Cleveland to see ducks on Easter.

We walked around the circular road for the Museum, and came out on top of the lagoon, looking down. Below us were hundreds of black girls with bright coats and purple corsages and patent leather shoes. Some had hats like we did, but the coolest had lots of bows, or braids with beads in their hair. Some carried minuscule pocketbooks over their arms. The boys looked good too, in their Sunday suits and ties. We glanced up at Dad. Even though we were dressed up, it didn't seem that we really belonged. But he just started us down the stairs.

When we got down there, Dad pushed Matt and me into the crowd. Cabot caught right up, Luke grabbed her hand. Egg Man walked on the outside, carrying Lucy.

And once you got started, you could see right away why people had done it for years. It was just nice, is all. The way we were all going in the same direction, with parents and children and grandparents all holding hands. And even when somebody was slower in front, nobody passed. But the second time we came full around, Dad had us step out of line.

Then the way he turned to look, we all did, up to the front of the big museum, and looming there, massive and monstrous but not in a bad way—there was *The Thinker*.

We looked at Dad because of Mother to see what we'd do. He told us to climb.

When we got to the top, Matt whispered, Awesome. Because Mother was right. *The Thinker* was bombed. He was missing half his face, much leg, and some arm. Yet he was still thinking. The bomb hadn't ruined him, it had improved him. You're a better thinker once you can think through a bomb.

Luke said, "Hey, Dad? What happened to him?"

Matt answered, "Dynamite."

Luke said, "Hey, Dad? What's he thinking?"

Matt answered, "He's thinking that someone blew him up with a bomb."

I said, "Why doesn't Mother like him? Because of the bomb?"

Dad didn't answer. But at least Matt didn't either.

Cabot said, "Don't worry about the bomb, everybody. It's still art."

Fact is, nobody was that worried about that part. But Cabot came here a lot, so she probably knew. She had lessons in drawing two times a week at the Cleveland Museum school. In the evenings. Dad took her. Mother didn't like the art lessons. They were downtown.

Dad said, "So tell us the artist, Cab."

"Rodin is."

We all stood in a half circle like a museum group and nodded.

Cabot said, "He's a sculptor."

We nodded.

Cabot said, "He's French, and he's dead."

We nodded.

"He had his first drawing lesson when he was ten years old. At age fourteen, he entered the Petite Ecole, as distinguished from the more prestigious Ecole des Beaux Arts, which wouldn't let him in there. *However* . . ."

Enough already. This was all about her. We broke ranks and started circling around.

Until now, I hadn't been thrilled with men statues before. They were usually on a horse, going to war. You had to worry so much for the horse. But I really did like *The Thinker*. I told Cabot another bomb could go off, and nothing would stop him. He'd think until he was just a heap of stone on the ground.

Cabot said, "But he's bronze."

"That doesn't bother me."

Then we stopped circling and stood there, regrouped around Egg Man. Matt asked him who put the bomb there and Luke asked him why.

After a long silence, during which he appeared to think about it almost as hard as *The Thinker* himself, Dad shifted Lucy to the other arm. And didn't answer. He just looked us all over, and then looked up the road, toward the car.

And that was it. It made you wonder why he'd brought us here if he didn't have anything to teach us. Even Cabot knew more.

We all stood there, holding our hats if we had them, and then, it was funny, but we all turned together to look back down at the pond. But below us, the paraders no longer looked festive. The sun was gone. It made the whole march look as if it had slowed right down.

"Okay," Egg Man said. "Back to the car."

We all looked around at one another, and all trudged off.

This time I sat up front, between Matt and Dad. Then we drove farther downtown, but only just cruising, and we had to keep asking, Seriously, Dad, in addition to a statue that was bombed, would we now see a river that burned.

But Dad wasn't talking. Though sometimes, like a man on a tour bus, he'd stop in front of big, fancy, gray buildings and announce their names out loud. "Athletic Club." "Union Club."

"Terminal Tower." We already knew the buildings, from other Easters, or from children's Christmas parties in these very places, if that's where they were. But we still liked when Dad stopped and announced things, very deep and slow and unnecessary, because it all told you he was joking around.

"Saint John's Cathedral," Dad intoned like a tour man.

The doors flung open and people started streaming out, hordes of them, in a hurry, maybe to go catch the parade at the pond. Waving good-bye to them all was a black preacher in golden robes at the top of the stairs. So maybe that's what reminded me of church that morning and social consciences. You could see the resemblance, is all that I'm saying, and suddenly I was asking, "Hey, Egg Man? Does Clarine have a conscience?"

He glanced down at me with a frown. "Clarine? Of course."

He was coaxing the Buick carefully through the church throng. But after he looked around at the people, he slowly wound up back at me. "Boyce," he said, "you're too smart to ask that."

"No I'm not." And Matt immediately backed me up on it.

Dad shoved the car into park and waited for the people to cross. "But why would you ask such a thing?"

I knew what he was thinking. That I'd asked because Clarine was a black person, and I felt like showing how stupid I was. Except that wasn't the reason I'd asked. I'd really asked because Clarine and I, we were both black sheep. I'd realized it that morning in church. Even so, there was something wrong with asking about Clarine when I was just afraid to ask for myself, and now I was ashamed. I hung my head and admitted, "I might have lapsed."

Dad leaned down closer and said, *"What?"*

"Never mind. I just can't find my conscience."

Matt laughed, but stopped when Dad snapped, "What's the question? Where's your conscience?"

The way he said it, I was scared.

"Well, is that the problem?"

"Right," I said, pulling the brim of my Easter hat down.

"Do you know what conscience is, or not?"

I didn't answer. I was mortified. Here I'd told a Protestant I'd lapsed.

Dad sat there tapping the steering wheel. Then Matt started drumming the dash, keeping time. Then Dad asked him, kind of quick and sharp, "Can *you* define conscience for us?"

"Uh, you mean you want, like, a definition?"

"Cabot?"

Dead silence all around.

Dad sat there tapping the steering wheel so long, I sensed, even with my head down, that now all of the people outside were gone, had already reached the parade at the pond.

Luke whispered to Cabot, "How come no one asked me?"

Dad yanked the Buick out of park, stepped on the gas, and, with a jolt, we took off.

It was like we were starting all over, and already, this was the ride we'd been hoping for all along.

Now he was driving fast and didn't make any announcements about things outside. We raced out to a highway where Lake Erie was, up the ramp, opened up on the road, took another ramp and got off. Matt announced "Fred's Fish Market" in a deep, brief voice, trying to make it sound like a tour man, but he only knew it because he read it from a big sign on stilts, and you could see right through that. Not that we still didn't like it, though. It was a total ruin. A wrecked old restaurant sitting way out at the end of a broken-down pier.

"Do we get to go there?" somebody asked.

Just looking at Fred's Fish Market cheered me up right off.

There were sailboats crossing back and forth on the water and there was a long metal barge that bobbed slowly along. Dad swung a right onto the pier. The wooden slats of the dock rumbled under the car as we thundered toward the end. This must be the place he was planning to take us all along. Right? The dirty lake? The source of the river that burns? I turned to check with Cabot. "Are we getting out of the car?"

Egg Man shook his head, Wrong. "But if you like it, Boyce," he said, "then take a brain picture."

I blinked up. "Really? How?"

"Just look at what you see and put it in your head and keep it there. Then, if you study it long enough, and let it develop over time, someday you might know something."

Well fine, but it would be a hell of a lot easier if he'd stop the car. Instead we rounded the end of the pier between Fred's Fish Market and the dock posts at about a hundred miles an hour. Everyone screams. Except Lucy. She laughs.

Two seconds later, back at the entrance to the pier, Dad careened another right. And even though the sun was setting behind us on the lake, and dusk was settling all around, he drove us deeper and deeper into downtown Cleveland.

He sped us past old, abandoned buildings, junkyards and shipping docks, traveling way beyond the point where Mother surely would have said to roll up the windows and lock the doors. He swung quick lefts and fast rights, winding us farther into a maze of streets you began to wonder how he would ever manage to wind us back out of. So deep into those streets, somewhere in there, it seemed we passed a sort of point of no return.

When he finally slowed up to sixty, we were in what looked to be almost a neighborhood. Except there was no grass. There were no yards. Some of the buildings had no doors. Without glass, the windows were blank, like eye sockets without eyes, so, unlike our house, there were no intricate reflections mirroring wind in the trees. But you could tell, there were still people living in there.

Because I'd never seen anything like it, I thought I should take some of those brain pictures Egg Man recommended before. So I tried it. But he hadn't taught me to do it right. Nothing was taking. I saw a bashed up old car showered in broken glass. But as quickly as I saw it, it passed. I saw a man who lay by the road under a mountain of dirty blankets, with a clean white dog in his arms. I saw a boy in a bright pink tee shirt, with nothing to match it, nothing else on, not even pants. They all came and they went. Except when I saw the old lady sitting smack on the sidewalk. She was wearing an Easter hat, but she wasn't wearing any shoes. She must have tried to get dressed up for Easter. But then she must have realized, What's the use, you can't parade without shoes. And you just knew what happened. She just sat down.

I looked at my own shoes, and back out at her. I swore this time I'd take a brain picture, and it might have even happened, maybe not in full living color, but I know I heard a sort of click inside. To test it, I closed my eyes, and she was still there in my mind. But as soon as we rounded the corner, she vanished, and even when I looked at my shoes to remind me, all I could see was just white socks and black shoes, like always before.

Now we were on another street. And this one was different from the others. Here there were three freshly painted white houses, huddled together like hope in the middle of the desolate block. That's when Egg Man finally hit the brakes and the Buick came to a total stop.

It was now as quiet as a church in the car.

We all sat there, eyes glued to our father. All in all, we all already knew, he had taken us far beyond a river that burns.

Then suddenly, without any warning, just like that, Egg Man started telling us things.

"See those three white houses?"

We all nodded. Each of us looked around to see if the others were looking the right way. But you already knew where to look, you only had to follow Dad's eyes.

"Well, they're bothering my conscience."

My eyes shot back from the three houses, to him.

"See, those three houses belong to me. To all of us, really. They were part of Father's estate. Before that, they were part of your great-grandfather's estate. The problem is, we haven't collected rent on those houses in about a hundred years. Nobody would do it because the people who live there are poor. So now I pay the up-keep and I pay the taxes. But in a year or two, that investment might finally pay off. Because a developer is planning to build a highway through here. I'll be able to sell those houses for a lot of money. Actually, for a lot more than they're worth, almost any price I ask."

He stopped, drew a cigarette from his pocket, lit it with the lighter in the dashboard, opened the window, and sent the smoke out.

He was smoking in front of us. He sent it out, casual and long. "And I'd like to do that, I really would. But if I do, what happens?"

Nobody really wanted to say it, the answer was too sad. But Dad said, "Cabot? What happens?"

"I think," she said, not wanting to say it, for sure. "Then the people won't have a house to live in anymore."

"That's right, Cab, they won't. And they can't afford to go somewhere else. They'll end up on the street."

Everybody was all quiet, all leaning forward a little, all staring out. Something like this, the place, the problem, him talking and smoking like he did with Mother or Clarine or his best friend Mr. Carter, had never really happened before in our lives.

"So, Boyce. Why don't you tell us what to do?"

"Me?" I scowled up at him. Ask Matt, he was oldest. Ask Cabot, she was smartest. The other two could talk.

"You." He pulled my hat off and tried to put it in my lap. But it was too big for that, so he handed it off to Matt, who bolted around about holding it like he'd been handed a bomb. But he did keep his mouth shut.

Then Dad said all I had to be was "brutally honest." I didn't have to be a hero. But then he added, "But better let your conscience be your guide."

Yeah, I got it. You knew what he was getting at.

So I looked out at those three white houses. Then I crossed my leg, put my elbow on my knee and my chin in my hand, and tried to think along the lines that *The Thinker* had.

But in the end, pure thinking let me down. Because all you had to do was stop thinking and look around. Your conscience wasn't in your brain. It wasn't in your stomach either. Or even in your heart. It was easier than that to find it. It was in your eyes.

Matt said, "Do we have this kind of time?"

I looked up at Egg Man. "May I decide in a year or two, please?"

He kind of laughed. "Listen. Say in a year or two, you can't really afford to give assets away. That will make your decision even harder. You can't just have a conscience when it's convenient. . . ." He sort of drifted off. When he snapped back, he said, "But as you say, we do have a year or two to decide." He opened the ashtray in the dashboard, pressed his cigarette out, and looked again at the three white houses with all of us. "Those people in there are old. Poor and old is a bad combination."

I couldn't even look at the three houses after that.

"Hell, our house only cost one dollar. Don't you remember?"

Of course. The memory was my first, and him saying it like that, gentle and everything, that went straight to my heart. "So are you going to do that and give them those three houses for a dollar, Dad?"

Cabot said, "Three dollars."

Dad said, "It's your call."

I pressed my lips together. I could still choose anything I wanted. I didn't have to be a hero. All I had to be was brutally honest. I closed my eyes.

I opened them when Matt slapped my hat in my lap. "I can't do it, Dad."

"Do what."

"Can't give the houses away for a dollar and can't sell them to the development man either. I think we should just leave it the same." Then I added timidly, "And maybe wait for the poor old people to die." There. There was your brutally honest.

Matt said, *"Man."*

Even Cabot gasped out loud.

Dad said, "Hmmm."

"Maybe we could take a brain picture," I said.

He looked down, distracted. "Huh?"

"You said someday we'd know something."

"Did I?" He stared down at me, I up at him, but for his part, he probably wasn't really looking, or he would have turned away. After winking or something. He twisted the key in the ignition and revved up the car.

That was it? What was he doing? Maybe I knew in that moment what an Egg Man was. How much mysterious power one had. Like fathers, when they were finished with you, they could just start the car.

Without further discussion, without answering questions, simply without elaboration at all, he drove us safely back through the maze of dirty streets that had gotten us there.

• • •

At Easter dinner that night, Mother was wearing her new ruby ring with pavé diamonds, an heirloom Dad stashed away when Grandfather died. She had decoded her clues successfully, and on the very first day. So she looked extra sparkling when she took a sip from her water glass. She held it up as if to toast someone special, which turned out to be us. She smiled at Luke. Everyone always smiled at Luke. "Did you see ducks, Lukie?"

Fork in midair, Luke looked as if he didn't know whether he'd been caught in the act, or what. But turns out, he just wasn't listening. "Yes, I like ducks."

Saw ducks, we all wanted to say, but sure didn't.

Mother looked down the table straight to Dad, as if shooting an arrow, but one of those soft, love ones. "And did we see anything else?"

Dad faked a frown, and steered her away as smooth as a Buick.

When Clarine served the Baked Alaska, I asked how you could cook ice cream in the oven and it would still come out like ice cream, and not like a pond.

At first, nobody was interested. I looked up at Mother. But she was helping Lucy so she wouldn't slop meringue all over the white damask tablecloth. So I looked down at Dad. "How, Dad?"

When he answered me, he was really looking at Mother. "Because it's insulated."

"What's *insulated?*"

But it was one of those things, like conscience, I guess, that even though you might ask, you sort of know what it is in your heart all along. Anyway, nobody answered.

So I looked down at Mother. Then back to Dad. And when he winked at me, I guess I got what the game really was. Rubies weren't the only treasures he'd been hiding from Mother. He had gone and hidden his conscience from her.

GIRLHOOD

Mother called a meeting for Catholics. It was held in the sitting room, and we all had to sit next to one another on the couch. Mother stood.

She said the purpose of the meeting was to tell us we would start having meetings that were called called Breakfast Meetings. She said she wanted a family that prayed together, and on Friday mornings, we should be prepared. And she set the time and the date for the first one. It was all very official. Then the meeting was over.

All I'm saying is, we had a meeting just to be told about more meetings. But Cabot said that's how it was done in the business world. After I heard that, I got pretty excited about it. I had to admit, it sounded good, to be able to have a Breakfast Meeting. I was pretty impressed with them, I guess.

The Friday of the first meeting, Cabot and I were almost late, because of our skating lesson.

Mother was late today too. She arrived in the dining room in a flowing red robe, which was a little unusual, because she was usually dressed up and everything, even at breakfast.

Dad stood up, she sat down, he went to the end of the table to get his kiss, getting a quick tap on the face this time instead. He went out to find the gray felt hat, Clarine came in, flung Mother her eggs sort of short-order style, and swung back through the swinging dining room door.

Except for the red robe, the quick tap, and no kiss, so far, business as usual.

Hat in hand, Dad made his traditional reappearance in the doorway. "So long, now," he said tentatively, surveying us cautiously, unsure why we were all still sitting there, hands folded on the table, lined up like a board meeting. "You won't be late for school?"

Mother blew a kiss and waved. "Bye, now."

He still stood there, on this day of all days, reluctant to go. So we all pitched in and cried "Bye, Daddy!!!" over and over, so it trilled in the halls like church bells and he was out the door and on his way to the four-car garage. Mother hadn't come right out and said so, but clearly the family that prayed together was to be kept secret from Dad.

When she heard a blue Buick leave the driveway, Mother flicked her fingernail on her crystal water glass. And called our first Breakfast Meeting to order.

My appointed seat at the table was to my father's left.

Mother had told me that this was the "guest of honor" position, but later I found out she had told Cabot hers was the guest-of-honor position, and Luke his was the guest-of-honor position, and when I finally consulted *Emily Post*, I learned that the official guest-of-honor position is to the head-of-the-table's right. And that seat, next to Dad, belonged to Matt. Naturally. He was a boy.

"I look like a boy. That should count for something," I'd complained to Cabot. But of course she was upset I'd just informed her she wasn't any guest of honor herself.

Anyway, that's how it had always been at the table, each of us having an appointed seat, each of us believing we were the guest of honor, and bound to our best decorum because of the big compliment.

But after Dad left for work that Friday of the first Breakfast Meeting, I slipped out of my chair and into his. From here, I had the best view of Mother. With her shoulder-length hair and flowing red robe, with my brothers and sisters lining the table like tiny apostles, she looked like one of those Last Supper paintings of Jesus, which sometimes make the Son of God look like a girl.

Mother flicked her fingernail on her crystal water glass. "Listen up, angels. The purpose of these meetings will be to organize our souls and learn to pray together to achieve our spiritual goals."

In other words, no more lapsing. She was planning to run a much tighter spiritual ship. You could tell. We were Catholic and she wanted to keep it that way. Plus she was probably making it up to God for sending us to private schools.

She stood up and went to the buffet table, where, from under the soft gray felt silverware cases there, she slipped something out. I sat up, trying to see. But whatever it was, it was tucked under her sleeve until she stood back at the end of the table.

Then she held up a stack of pamphlets. "These are for you to keep, and you must take care of them. Each of you gets six. Cabbie, count six for yourself and pass the rest down."

Cabot said, "What about Lucy?"

In the high chair next to Cabot sat Lucy, another former guest of honor.

Mother nodded. "She'll like the pictures."

So Cabot counted six pamphlets for herself, then six more for Lucy, and passed the rest down. Lucy set them out on the tray of her high chair, then launched them one by one to the floor.

When I got mine, I saw they were prayer pamphlets. On the covers, they had pictures of saints, all with halos on their heads. Some had things like lions and eagles riding on their shoulders, or falcons in the palms of their hands. They were very unusual. I looked up at Mother. She must have bought a religion store.

She nodded at me to hurry the process along. I quickly counted six and passed the rest to Matt. He gave me a look, but I didn't look back.

Mother flicked her water glass. "I don't want you reading these now. But I'd like you to study them later, in your rooms. We're going to be deciding on something to pray for, as a unit."

Matt said, "You mean like a family unit? Something like that?"

"Yes, like a family unit."

"Oh. Just asking."

"Straighten up, Matt."

Cabot said, "No slouching," which was completely unnecessary, since Mother had already said straighten up. Besides, it just made Matt sink farther down.

Mother flicked her water glass. "Now, you all know what a novena is, don't you?"

We looked around at each other, unsure.

Cabot said, "They do."

"Would you like to refresh their memories, Cab?"

In a snooty, singsong voice, Cabot said, "A novena is a series of prayers recited to a single saint every day for nine straight days in a row."

Matt and I looked at each other. Jesus.

Mother said, "Each of your six pamphlets represents a novena to one special saint. I'd like you to read them all privately in your rooms, then we'll meet again next Friday and pick a saint together, and pray for something together, as a happy family."

Matt said, "A happy family *unit*, right?" He looked around at the rest of us, "Remember, not just a happy family, you guys. A happy family *unit*."

Cabot said, "Could someone please get him to stop saying family unit like that?"

Mother flicked her water glass, which now sounded like: Children. "All right. Now, before we adjourn for school, let's start thinking of something to pray for together, as a family." Faster than Matt could say family unit, she added, "Any ideas?"

Luke said, "You mean we're giving up on Dad?" For some time now we'd been told to pray to St. Anthony, Patron Saint of Lost Things, to ask God to help Dad and Clarine "find" the Catholic Church.

Mother said, "No, no dear. I just thought it might be nice to think of something new, something fresh, to pray for."

We all looked around at one another. The fact is, I think we liked praying to St. Anthony that Dad and Clarine find a church. It was familiar territory. This new happy family thing sounded hard.

Mother said, "So now let's take a minute, be devout, and search our souls."

After looking around to see how to do it, everybody took a minute and pretended they were doing it.

"Okay. Let's hear some suggestions."

Luke raised his hand. "How about bowling balls? We don't have any of those."

Cabot and I glanced at each other. But Mother seemed to consider it. She pursed her lips and frowned, which was her way of showing Luke it had been a real tough choice, about the bowling balls, but . . . no. "Honey, God can easily grant us a bowling ball. But wouldn't it be better to pray for something a little more holy than a bowling ball?"

Cabot giggled. "That's funny. More *holey* than a bowling ball." She looked around. "Get it?"

It took a while. Then I said, "Get it everybody? Much more *holy* than a bowling ball." I looked at Luke. "A bowling ball's not holy, Luke."

Cabot said, "A bowling ball has *holes*, Luke."

Luke's face suddenly lit up like Christmas.

Matt whispered, "God."

"Girls." Mother tapped her water glass.

I raised my hand. "How about a blue Buick?" Not too original, no, but tried and true. Plus, she'd probably go for it, and then we could go to school.

Matt snorted, "I'm not praying for any Buick." He was fifteen now, and probably hoping we'd pray for Porsches. But he didn't say so, instead he straightened up and said, very maturely, as if he were suddenly wearing a three-piece suit and a silk tie, "I'd like everyone to do it for boxing gloves."

Cabot said, "That sure sounds more holy than a bowling ball."

Mother's mouth was suddenly all pressed together. "Matt, and when did you develop this desire for boxing gloves?"

"I've always had it! I've said it a million times! I think I'll go crazy if I don't get some soon!"

First I'd heard of it. But I believed him. He looked a little on the edge right now.

"Ask Dad! He *listens*!"

Mother narrowed her eyes. A lot, so he'd know. "Well, Matt, I've told you. I don't want you boxing. Under no circumstances do I want you to box. Ever. Never. Period."

Matt crossed his arms and sank down so far he almost slid right under the table.

It had been a while since the last Easter drive with Dad. We hadn't gone this past year because of spring skiing. But I still remembered certain things that I'd seen. I raised my hand. "Poor people?"

Mother looked genuinely impressed. "Praying for poor people. Well, that idea has some merit. Let's all think about that for next week. And everyone think up his own idea too. Then we'll decide together, as a family. Any questions?"

Matt raised his hand.

Cabot said, "He's going to say family unit again."

Mother immediately flicked her water glass. "Okay, angels. Meeting adjourned."

Clarine barged in to clear the dishes. You could tell. She thought our Breakfast Meeting was for the birds.

But I didn't. I thought they were good. Cabot complained they were a bureaucratic nightmare, not unlike the Catholic Church itself, she said, but I was more inclined to look at the bright side, because they were Breakfast Meetings and all. Maybe I wasn't so lapsed as I thought I was. Or maybe I was relapsing, from my lapse. Either way, I was pleased about my idea to pray for poor people. That way, maybe God would do something, so Dad wouldn't have to. In fact, if we kept these meetings up, maybe we wouldn't have to give houses away for a dollar and such, and then we'd never have to be poor ourselves.

That night, I did as instructed and studied my prayer pamphlets in my room. Then I laid them all out on my bed, with the picture sides up, so I could see all the interesting things saints carried around. "Hello, angel."

I looked up. Mother had quietly arrived in my doorway to watch. "Aren't they special?"

You would have to say, they were special. I knew for a fact I was the only kid on the block with prayer pamphlets. I picked up Saint Anthony. "These are good pictures," I said.

Tall, slim, and balding, Saint Anthony was depicted holding the Christ Child, his eyes rolled way up to heaven, as if he were either really drunk or incredibly bored. I put Saint Anthony down, and lifted Saint Francis. Of them all, Francis was easily the sweetest saint, pictured smilingly surrounded by smiling little birds, smiling little flowers, smiling little clouds, and smiling little, floating lambs. I put Saint Francis down and considered Saint Jude. He was portrayed as macho-saint, with his hair slicked back and one eyebrow raised and one finger cocked toward heaven like a pistol.

Mother said, "He's the Patron Saint of Hopeless Cases."

I didn't know they had their own saint. I picked up my favorite pamphlet. "I like this saint the best."

"Really, dear? Why?"

"She's the prettiest."

"Well, yes, she was very beautiful. That's Saint Theresa of the Little Flower. She was so modest and loving and pure, like a lovely little flower, they nicknamed her 'The Little Flower.'"

She was very, very pretty. Even in the brown nun's habit she wore. "She married Jesus."

"Oh. But, no. She really didn't."

But it said so inside. I'd read it three times. I held it out, so Mother could see.

" 'By becoming a sister.' See? Saint Theresa's marriage to Jesus was a 'pure' marriage, dear. When a sister becomes a sister, it's called marrying God. But there's just a tiny little difference between that kind of marriage and the one your father and I have. You'll learn all about it when you grow up."

I already knew enough about the tiny little difference not to talk to her about it. I pored over my pamphlet.

Saint Theresa was shown hovering a few feet above the world. She had the brown nun's habit, which wasn't at all attractive, far worse than black, but she had graceful arms, which she held extended, and from her hands fell hundreds of red roses.

Mother sat on the edge of my bed. "Saint Theresa died at a very young age. All her life, she loved flowers. Before she died, she promised to send what she called 'a shower of roses' from heaven to earth. So if you pray to Saint Theresa, and she talks to God about it, and He decides to grant your prayer, Saint Theresa will let you know by sending you a single red rose. That is her sign."

I looked up. "Her what?"

"Sign. It means she'll let you know if your prayer will be answered. Someone on earth will hand you a single red rose."

"Really?" This was maybe the best thing I had heard in my life. For the first time, you could pray, and actually know if you would get what you wanted, or were just totally wasting your time.

Mother winked. "Really."

Really? Suddenly I didn't feel like waiting for Friday anymore. I opened the pamphlet. "O holy Saint Theresa of the Little Flower . . ."

Mother put her hand on my arm. "But what are you praying for, dear?"

"To be as pretty as *she* is."

Mother smiled and shook her head sort of sadly. "It's not enough to be as pretty. You must also pray to be as modest, as loving, and as pure."

That didn't sound like it looked very good.

"Just put 'pretty' last. Pretty isn't so important."

Easy for her to say. She looked like Saint Theresa. "Do I have to?" Naturally, I was worried that if I put pretty last, Saint Theresa would mistakenly think it was the least important. And if she decided to answer just some of my prayers, and hold something back to teach me a lesson or something dreadful like that, you just know what would go. "Are you going to make me?"

"Yes, yes. These are called 'priorities.' You must always be very careful about the order of your priorities. Pretty goes last."

Damn. But what could I do. So before Mother turned off the lights, we recited all the prayers in Saint Theresa's novena pamphlet, asking, when the request what you want here part came up, that I become modest, loving, pure, and *Pretty*. Which I have to admit, I yelled pretty loud.

"Listen up, angels."

It was Friday, Dad was safely down the driveway, so we got straight down to business. But it simply took time. We had to go all around the table, hearing every last lame suggestion for what to pray for as a family. Matt whined about boxing gloves again, and I lobbied for poor people. A few other things mentioned included household pets, helicopters, and Luke's special request—his own box seats to the Cleveland Browns so he could take all his friends. To that, Matt grumbled, "Get a problem." We ended again without finding anything. "Sorry angels, meeting adjourned."

I'm not going to mention every last Breakfast Meeting. But we were losing heart. Mother didn't think anything was good enough to pray for as a family. But finally, one Friday, it happened. It was the week Luke stopped asking if we could all pray to God that he get his own box seats to the Cleveland Browns and blurted, "Okay, I lied. I don't want box seats. I don't want to *go* there. I want to *play* there. I want to *be* a Cleveland Brown."

We all looked at Mother. Surprisingly, she didn't say no. She nodded and said, "Cabot?"

Catching on rather quickly, I have to admit, Cabot said, "Uh, I want to be an artist who makes big statues to sit outside major museums?"

We all looked at Mother. She didn't say no. She nodded and said, "Boyce?"

So, jumping on the old bandwagon, I said, "I wouldn't mind winning three gold medals in the Olympics for figure skating."

When we all looked at Mother, once again, she didn't say no. She nodded thoughtfully and said, "Matt?"

Blinking as if he'd just been crowned king for a day, Matt sat up ramrod straight. "Heavyweight Champion of the World!"

Mother narrowed her eyes so not only he'd know, but so he'd remember for life. "Matt, I don't want you boxing. Never. Ever. Not ever at all."

So maybe in due time, Luke would have become a Cleveland Brown, Cabot a famous artist, and me an Olympic champion, if Matt hadn't recovered lost ground immediately by sullenly changing his request from Heavyweight Champion of the World to, "Okay, then just president of the United States of America."

We all looked at Mother. Oh, *no*.

So, extremely grudgingly, and I mean grudgingly in the extreme, we all agreed to pray Matt into the United States presidency. Except Mother said make it class president for starters, and Matt had a deal.

I had no intention of making Matt president if God wasn't going to do something about making me pretty, and of course poor people too. So I started saying double and triple prayers to Saint Theresa on the side. If Mother stopped by at bedtime, she found me praying. And she'd kneel down to join me. It became our little secret.

I began to hope for The Sign of the single red rose the way most people hope for The Sign of winning the lottery. And at times the chance of receiving one single red rose seemed just as what's called "mathematically improbable." Because it didn't count if someone handed you a dozen red roses or a single yellow rose or any roses buried in a box from the florist. The way Saint Theresa had set The Sign up with God, someone had to *hand* you a *single*, *red* rose. Those three things, in that order, or else.

It dawned on me one day that a person could live an entire lifetime and never have this perfect combination happen. That night, I expressed my concerns to my mother. She told me that God helps those. So we decided to help ourselves.

The next morning, we took Lucy for a walk in the garden. None of us were allowed to pick the flowers without permission, and Lucy was growing to understand this as well as any of us. But while we must, in good conscience, teach Lucy the house rules, we could still afford to indulge her natural instincts as a child. So when she toddled up to the tulips and said, "Pretty!" I said, "Yes, Lucy, 'pretty,' but don't touch."

And when she sat in front of the irises and said, "Flower!" Mother said, "Yes, sweetie, 'flower,' but don't pick."

But when she ran to the rosebush and said, *"Red!"* neither Mother nor I said a damn thing. We looked at the sky. We talked about the weather. We ignored Lucy with our whole hearts and prayed to God she would follow the simple, innocent, childlike impulse to pick a *single red rose* and *hand* it to her sister or mother. But all Lucy would do was stand there yelling *"Red!"*

Meanwhile, miraculously, Matt started shaping up as the perfect presidential candidate. He grew more handsome, more personable, and even more eloquent. Unfortunately, in the time-honored political tradition, he also began to lie, cheat, and steal. Dressed as Honest Abe Lincoln, he won a mock presidential debate at school. But then Matt failed to register as a candidate for class president on the day he was supposed to. On that day, he slipped out of school and spent the afternoon at a seedy downtown gym, slugging a heavy bag in a ripped-off pair of boxing gloves.

The fact that Matt was not only not a presidential candidate but also a truant, a boxer, and a thief naturally didn't help matters any. He had to return the boxing gloves he'd "borrowed" from Big Al's

Sporting Goods Store, plus he had to pay for them out of his own savings account. In the Catholic Church, this is called doing "penance."

But Big Al wouldn't take Matt's penance. Cabot and I thought it was pretty strange to go to a store and try to pay for something that you'd already stolen and already slipped back on the shelf. I guess Big Al thought it was pretty strange too, because he wouldn't take Matt's savings. So Dad and Mother and Big Al and Matt all got together and decided to donate the money, plus some, to a boys' correctional institute's sports program, which happened to be very big on boxing.

I'm sure Matt would have gladly furthered his career as a juvenile delinquent just so he could land in that boys' correctional institute with the well-endowed boxing program, but I guess he was saved by the grace of God. Because shortly after the crime, a series of big brown boxes arrived from UPS, addressed to Dad. When he came home from work, Mother said, "George? What's in those big boxes?"

Dad said, "Matt's boxing equipment."

We all lined up to watch their first big fight, now taking place behind the closed library door.

It was an almost festive atmosphere. Luke went to the kitchen to get home-baked sugar cookies from Clarine, so we even had snacks. We sat and ate them on the front stairs. As self-appointed ringmaster or something, Cabot repeatedly went to the library door and listened, reporting back, "She says she wants him to be class president." "She says what good will it do him, they don't have boxing in the Ivy League anymore." The whole time, Matt stood in the corner biting his nails, which didn't make him look very fierce like a boxer at all.

After an hour or so, it quieted down in the library, and Cabot came back with a nervous look on her face, like maybe Dad was in there, knocked out on the floor. But when the library doors opened, Dad said, "Okay, Matt. Let's take these downstairs."

Punch drunk from his sudden change in fortune, Matt tore through the boxes right there in the hall. He got not just boxing gloves but a speed bag and a heavy bag and a double-end bag too. "Boy oh boy!" he cried at the last box. "Look, you guys! My very own crazy bag!"

Cabot peeked into the box. "Is that what this one's called?"

He looked at her like a maniac. "Yeah!"

"Just checking."

Then Matt glanced at the ceiling and smiled the serene smile of one who has just learned firsthand that crime, not to mention sin, does in fact pay. Wearing this mug, he glided behind Dad to the basement, where they spent the evening installing the boxing equipment in the sort of gym down there.

A few days later, after school, Matt approached me in the breakfast room. "Hi, Zu," he said, very friendly.

"Hi."

"So how's school, little sis?"

Little sis? What was this? I said it was fine.

"That's great." He did a little one-two punch for emphasis in the air. "That's tremendous."

I was having a leftover sugar cookie. I held up the plate, but he said he was in training. And he did a little shuffle, and punched at nothing some more. Then he stopped dancing around the room and got serious. "You know, I was thinking, you're only a little girl. You need to learn self-defense."

Oh. He needed a sparring partner.

I said, "Don't butter me up to box with you, because I don't like the basement."

He said, "You don't like the *basement?*" As if he'd never heard of it before.

"Remember? The subconscious? Well, I don't like it too much, Matt." He himself had told us that every house has a subconscious, which is the part below ground, and evil things you can't even imagine happen down there. Don't get me wrong, we all knew he'd said it just so he could have the basement all to himself, but the way he made our subconscious sound, he had it. The rest of us couldn't go down there without clutching the hand of Dad or Clarine.

"The basement is *beautiful.*"

"You just need someone to box with."

"So? Don't be such a girl."

That made me mad enough to go learn to box, so next time I could defend myself against people like him. He taught me to do things like hook, jab, and slip a punch. Then he gave me the title of "probably the best female flyweight girl-boxer in the world."

But even though I was proud of my title and all, I still thought the whole thing slightly suspicious from a theological standpoint. It seemed that if you asked God to make you president, what He did was make you, not to mention your sister, boxers instead.

After Matt's crime, we really buckled down at our Breakfast Meetings. Having blamed Matt's failure to become a likely candidate for president, and his unlikely success at becoming a boxer, on the fact that she hadn't taught us to pray hard enough, Mother began to mastermind nine-day novenas to three, four, as many as six saints at once. To keep track of it all, Mother decided to appoint a "secretary," really just a glorified scorekeeper. Still, I was thrilled when she offered me my very first job.

Our Breakfast Meetings became more purposeful, more organized, more businesslike. Once Dad was safely down the driveway, once Clarine barged out the swinging dining room door, the table came to order.

"Boyce, dear, what novena days are we on?"

"I've got the minutes here, Mother." My brothers and sisters waited while I unfolded my notes, which I'd hidden under my thigh until Dad and Clarine, the Protestants, were gone. "Four for Saint Anthony. Two for The Little Flower. Ninth day on Saint Anne. We finished Saint Francis yesterday, and we begin today on Little Claire." And all the while, I was also praying to Saint Theresa to be pretty, and to make poor people unpoor.

The funny thing is, not long after Matt's boxing equipment arrived, I realized Mother was also praying to Saint Theresa on the side. See, for weeks after the first big fight, she had been in a mood. I'd overheard complaints confided to Clarine. She'd say, "It's not really a sport, you know."

And Clarine would say, "Well, but it'll teach him to stick up for himself."

And Mother would look at Clarine as if to say, "When will he ever need to, in the Ivy League?"

Dad picked up on Mother's mood quite fast. He brought candy, he brought flowers. But the one thing he wouldn't bring was the one thing she probably was praying for: the boxing equipment back to Big Al's Sporting Goods Store.

I was sitting in the sunroom with Mother the evening Dad brought roses home. He had already tried the more exotic bouquets and New Age–looking arrangements, flowers that looked as if they'd led a wild, avant-garde sort of life on some chic, cold other planet. So now he was giving good old long-stemmed roses a whirl. When he brought them, they weren't even in a box. They were in a bunch, in his hand.

"Darling," Mother said, fairly convincingly, though not exactly jumping out of her chair. "Yellow roses!"

She sent me to the kitchen to get a vase from Clarine. I rushed back with it, splashing water over the rugs in my haste. We then arranged the flowers the way Mother had learned to in her flower-arranging class. "The man, the earth, and the sky," she said, clipping the last three yellow roses. "You cut some short, and that's the earth. You cut some medium, and that's the man. You cut some tall, and that's the sky."

"Why?"

"Just universality," she said, first shrugging, then stopping to stare into space. "Just grace."

When the flowers were all done and duly admired, Mother suggested a stroll with Dad in the garden.

I walked between them. It was something that was sometimes done, go with them to the garden before dinner, and the way they did it, they walked up to a particular bed of flowers, said things to each other about its progress, and then they just moved along. But tonight, after they did the red roses, Mother didn't move along. Instead she grabbed Dad's hand, sort of spun him around, and planted a big kiss on his mouth. When it finally ended, she drew back and said, "Darling? The yellow roses you brought me are beautiful. Yellow roses mean happy love. But red roses mean passionate love." A cloud crossed her radiant face. "George? Isn't our love passionate anymore?"

Now, most men can take a hint if you slap them in the face with it. And so could Dad. But most men would have simply reached down, broken off a single red rose, and forked it over. But not

Dad. He wanted to declare their love was still passionate, but I guess he wanted to do it up proud. So when Mother finally gave up on him and went in to dress for dinner, he started whacking red roses off the bushes by the dozen. I followed him in horror back into the house. He got us all in the dining room and let us in on the secret. Mutely, I watched as he dumped the mountain of roses right on top of her plate.

We heard her come rustling down the stairs and dove for our seats. She entered the room and stopped cold. Two spots of red flashed to her face. "George!" she said, blushing so deeply and so beautifully that not one of them could have guessed it was not pleasure that heightened her color. I knew it was something else entirely. The infinite frustration of trying to get handed a single red rose.

The next Friday, we Catholics met at breakfast, as usual. Mother wore the red robe, as usual. Dad stood up, kissed her good-bye, as usual. Returned with the hat, looking perplexed, as usual. Clarine swiped his plate and tossed Mother hers, as usual, and barged back out, all as usual. Then Mother opened the meeting with, what else, business as usual.

"Will the secretary please read what novena days we are on?"

"I've got the minutes here, Mother." Everyone sat up and waited while I unfolded my notes. "Eight for Saint Anthony. Three for Jude. Sixth day on Saint Anne. We start today again on Francis, and we might want to take another crack at Saint Claire."

"Very good." Mother nodded from the other end of the table. She smiled and looked around at all her guests of honor. "Are you all clear about that, or would you like Boyce to read the minutes one last time?"

One last time? Why had she said that? That was unusual.

But they all agreed they were all clear about it.

"I have a proposal," Mother then said. "Boyce has been the secretary for some time now and I think it only fair we let someone else try his or her hand at the job."

Dead silence. Everyone looked at me. I looked at my mother.

"Cabot," Mother continued, "has asked if she may apply for the position. I think she'd be able to handle it, but I would like to put it to a vote."

Dead silence. Everyone looked at Cabot. Cabot smiled modestly, behind her pure blond hair. Then, to my astonishment, every little hand in the room shot into the air, including Cabot's. My heart started thumping wildly against a cage in my chest. I looked at Lucy. She was voting twice, that is, with two hands, with a piece of toast in each, but she probably just liked to vote. But even if she were disqualified, there were still an awful lot of hands.

Mother said, "All opposed?"

I sat there, clutching my minutes to my pounding chest. I couldn't even vote.

"Boyce, dear. Would you please give Cabot the minutes? She will be the secretary from now on."

I folded my arms and hung my chin to my chest. I began kicking under the table as if I was skating to get away.

"Boyce," Mother said, "please give Cabot the minutes."

If this were some lesson in Catholicism, it wasn't working. I crumpled my minutes and stuffed them right back under my thigh.

"Boyce? Please give Cabbie those minutes. Now."

I skated a long way before answering. I wanted to choose my words carefully. The forbidden "No way" is what I finally chose.

Everyone gasped.

"She said no way!" cried Matt.

"Quiet, Matthew." Then Mother asked me again. "Boyce, please give Cabot the minutes."

Skating faster and faster, I repeated my answer. "No way."

"Boyce Parkman. *What* did you say ?"

As if turning on a dime, I said, "I said *NO!!!*"

This was like the cock crowing three times when Judas Iscariot betrayed Jesus Christ. Except it was I who was being betrayed here, and in no way shape or form was I going to let them crucify me. In fact, I was going to stick up for myself.

I grabbed my minutes and made a flying camel for the door. Matt flew from his chair, lunged for my ankles, and toppled me to the floor. I rolled away. Then we were standing up. Then we were squaring off. Then we were dropping our chins. Then we were pronating our wrists. Then we were going to Sunday punch each other.

Except before we actually connected, Mother had sprung from her chair and Clarine had come steaming like a ring referee on speed skates through the swinging dining room door.

"I've had just about enough of this," she said, picking Matt off me and tossing him aside like a used towel. She grabbed the tattered minutes, and held them high in the air.

"I'll take that, Clarine." Mother made a swift pass and snatched the minutes out of Clarine's hand. "They're fighting over . . . schoolwork."

My mouth fell open. That was a *lie*.

And it was just then that we heard the whir of a car in the driveway. We all turned to look out the window. Then we all spun back around to look at Mother, even Clarine.

Matt and I dove for our seats. Clarine went back through the swinging door, and when it swung back in, Dad was standing there, frowning at us. "Forgot my case," he said. We sat, hands folded on the table, lined up like a board meeting. "Everything okay?"

It was my chance. I knew it. I could tell the truth, and he would defend it. But when I looked at Mother, I no longer knew what was right and what was wrong anymore. And then of course the moment passed.

Dad went down the hall and came back with his case. "Well, I guess I'm off to slay the dragon again." He said that sometimes. When I was little, I thought it was what he did for a living. "Bye, then," he said, and stood there a second longer before he shook his head a little and left.

When the Buick was down the driveway, Mother handed the minutes to me. I then had to stand up and walk around the table and hand them to Cabot. In total silence and absolute humiliation, I accomplished this. Immediately, either from joy or from terror, Cabot burst out crying.

I could have lived with it. I really could have. I might have even learned from it. I might have learned lessons about selflessness, fair play, sharing. Stuff that was truly good to learn. I might have even learned one of the great lessons of the Catholic Church, to "turn the other cheek." I might have. If it hadn't been for one simple, innocent, childlike gesture of Luke's.

See, when Cabot cried, Luke felt bad. He leaned over from his chair and patted her shoulder to make her stop. But that just made Cabot cry harder. So Luke tried kissing her arm. That made Cabot degenerate into sobs. So, in a final, Hail Mary effort to cheer her up, Luke stood on his chair, flung himself facedown on the table, and tackled the centerpiece. In the center of the centerpiece was one, single, red rose.

Before I had time to pounce on him, pummel him, kill him if

necessary, Luke plucked the flower and threw himself back across the dining room table, landing, elbows bent, in Cabot's plate. Covered with old breakfast but still clutching the single red rose, clutching it like it was the ball and he was a Brown and this was his winning touchdown in the final seconds of the Superbowl, he handed it to her.

Cabot's sobbing stopped midsob. Her eyes lit up. She took the rose and smiled prettily, not to mention modestly, lovingly, and purely.

It was not a huge leap to assume, then, that somewhere in the world at some other Breakfast Meeting, the rich had just gotten richer, and those poor people downtown were still poor.

I stopped attending Breakfast Meetings, claiming I had pressing business elsewhere. Now that I'd been nominated for class president at school.

THIRTEEN

It was a black day and I don't know why anybody would want
to hear about it, but it was a Saturday in summer, and I was sitting
on my bed with a cast and a crutch, writing a kind of letter in my
head, to my grandfather, who I already said was dead.

I guess I just felt like letting him know what I thought of Canadian tennis is all. Also, I owed him a thank-you note, for the pearls
he had given my father to give me when I turned thirteen, which
was my birthday, the day before.

I knew it was crazy to write him the letter, even in my head, but
I still started doing it anyway, mostly complaining about Canadian
tennis, because it has three players, and though you do get a partner, then you have to switch off, so your partner becomes your
opponent and then your opponent becomes your partner again. All
I'm saying is, you shouldn't trust anyone in Canadian tennis. I really
started to complain about it to my grandfather, saying what a sorry
excuse for an export Canada had. How once they came up with the
bacon and the quarters, maybe they should have quit while they
were ahead. I also asked my grandfather to check on a few other
countries, including our own, now that he could see the whole
world from the vantage point of heaven, that is if there is a God.

I started in the morning, and it got to be quite an elaborate letter
by later on. The first thing, when I woke up and found out I was

wearing my pearls with my pajamas, I just began. I told my grandfather how I had played Canadian tennis on my birthday, with my
two best friends, the two Mickeys. How when we switched part-
ners my knee went numb, but I kept playing like a madman anyway, and then when I fell down and got up and then fell down
again, the two Mickeys came and stood over me in their tennis
skirts and Mickey said, Hey, maybe I had to go to the hospital or
something. Which, when my Mother arrived in her golf skirt, is
what we did.

At the hospital, they gave me a cast and a crutch to walk around
on, then told me not to walk around.

The Mickeys bought me presents at the gift shop, including a
Seventeen magazine, and Mother pretended not to notice it, I guess
rewarding me for not crying too loud when the doctor turned my
kneecap back around. Now I was on my bed, and I'd been staring
at the cover of the *Seventeen* for about an hour. I was just getting
incredibly stubborn about starting it. I told my grandfather I
sometimes get perverse like that, wanting something all my life,
then thinking, This isn't exactly philosophy, now that I have my
hands on a copy. Besides, it was too quiet to read it. Dad was down
there in his library with the door closed.

I told my grandfather it was a Saturday in summer, and I was all
alone in the house with Dad. But I tried not to say too much about
that one, because Dad was his son and I didn't want to blame my
grandfather for him.

I also told my grandfather he may want to have a meeting about
eliminating the thirteenth birthday along with Canadian tennis. I
suggested they try what they do in some tall buildings, when the
elevator skips you straight from twelve to fourteen. And nobody
has to worry they've landed on the most unlucky floor.

Anyway, the advantage to this kind of letter is you can do it all day long. There's no time limit. It's not as if you have to get it to the post office or something, or have it ready for when the mailman comes. Also, you don't have to go in logical order, and there's not a lot of extra explaining to do. The person in heaven, that is if there is one, already knows the past and the future. Like Grandfather knew that I would get the message from Mickey Knight that day that I wasn't too beautiful at the moment, and how Dad would get the envelope back in the mail, and how I would solve the issue of world poverty, just not for very long. It made it easier to write the letter, because my grandfather already knew it was going to be a disappointing day all around.

I did it anyway, despite what the doctor said.

I took my crutch and got off my bed and hopped out to check on the library door. I wanted to do it quickly, and be back in my room in case Mickey Knight came to give me the makeover, which is something you learn in magazines, how to get instantly trans-formed from an ugly duckling into a swan. It was almost the first thing Mickey said when she saw my cast and my crutch. "Oh my God. I am so giving you a Before and After after this."

I got to the landing and stared down at the library door. I was beginning to feel I was the first in the family to ever be alone in the house with Dad. The silence was total. You could hear a knee crack.

He must be in there thinking something elevated, I thought. I decided I should do that too, you know, go back to my room and emulate. Why else would you have a Dad.

Then I had this idea to go down to the library, hop in, and just plop myself down. You see someone come in on a crutch, and what can you do. I debated it, I really did. Debated whether to be brave enough to interrupt Dad. Then I felt kind of silly, just stand-ing there staring at the door, with a crutch no less, like one of those beggars they won't let in church because nobody wants them around while they pray. So I gave up and hopped back to my room, determined to emulate once I got to my bed.

But on my bed, there was the *Seventeen*. So I sat in my chair.

My grandfather already knew: my two best friends already were Afters. Mickey Joslyn, who we called Jo, and Mickey Knight, who was actually born more of a Before. We lived within six blocks of one another.

Jo was beautiful. She had those pure, angelic looks that made her fine blond hair as radiant as a halo and her big blue eyes as round, innocent, and fathomable as country club baby pools. Mickey Knight wasn't, but wanted to be, as beautiful as Jo, the other Mickey. Mickey Knight's parents wanted that too. So they redid their daughter. Doctors redid her nose and chin, stylists bleached her hair, and opticians made her special contact lenses to brighten up her hazel eyes. So Mickey and Mickey ended up looking almost like twins. And I was the only remaining Before.

But that's not what I wanted to think about now. It wasn't elevated, it was almost the opposite. I decided to try my other armchair, even though I had the cast and it was clear across the room. On my way over, I stopped at the dresser and looked in the mirror, wondering how Mickey was going to do it, turn me from looking like a boy into a miniature movie star like she was. I still had that kind of crew cut Mother had always assured me was "darling." Other than that, I had a few freckles. Maybe I looked like Huck Finn. Or if he had a sister. I went to my other armchair and settled in, determined to forget about it and emulate Dad.

It was a good idea, to change chairs. Because the minute I got there I got the idea. I would just *end* poverty. I'd think up a solution. That way I wouldn't have to worry about it anymore.

Particularly, I thought I should work on world hunger. I had heard the phrase a lot, and it was easy enough to figure out what it meant. It meant that somewhere in the world, even as I debated which armchair to choose, people were starving.

After contemplating the subject for almost an entire half hour, I felt I had moved beyond mere comprehension of the facts. I had moved so far beyond that, I felt I was on the verge of a sort of revelation, and was beginning to believe if I just thought long and hard enough about world hunger, I would definitely solve the problem. Through sheer force of will, my mind would become one with the cure. So sitting there, I guess I reached a state as close as I'd ever come to true prayer.

But then, at the very second I figured out how to make everyone rich, the screech of tires shattered my thoughts.

I got up and hopped to the window. But it wasn't Mickey Knight down there. It was the blue-and-white mail truck. And Andrew John Hague, our postman, was climbing out, toting an envelope.

The bell rang. I hobbled out to the landing and hung back, waiting to see what Dad would do. And when the bell rang again, the library door did click open and I saw his battered old canvas shoes stride into view before I pulled back, out of sight. Then I sat down on the landing with my cast out straight and looked through the spokes of the railing, just in time to see the thick manila envelope change hands.

You would think Andrew John would have left promptly, having already delivered the mail. But he didn't. Instead, he attempted the impossible, or at least the unlikely—that is, small talk with my father. When this failed, he just sort of hung out down there, watching Dad receive his envelope, which Dad felt pressed to do more than the customary one time only. Dad kept reenacting this routine which meant, Thank you for bringing me this envelope. See? I have the envelope. Nice day, fat envelope. Thank you for delivering the mail, Andrew John, but why are you still here?

Andrew John stayed. It was a prolonged awkward moment. Dad wanted to get on with his envelope, but Andrew John apparently had something he wanted to add to that. Finally, he found a way. Reaching adroitly to take a corner of the envelope, Andrew John positioned himself beside my father, as if about to share a menu or a map. Then, pointing to the postmark, he said, "It's strange how they always come back in a month, to the day. I wonder if that's why they call it the 'Monthly.' You know, the *Atlantic Monthly?*"

Dad's eyebrows arched up. "You don't say."

"I'm a rejected writer myself, sir." Andrew John beamed.

No reaction this time from Dad, but as for me, I found the news disturbing. Dad held his envelope bravely while Andrew John talked about modern fiction and poetry. Then he offered to recite some of his own for my father. Without waiting for the okay, he launched into it in a great, booming voice and when it was over, he bowed deeply, turned suddenly, and left. There was a resounding silence in the hall.

I peered down at my father. "Daddy? Did something tragic just happen?"

But he just laughed up at me. "Zu, your head's too big to fit through that railing. Someday, you might lose it." And he made that jokey gesture where you clutch your throat and bulge your eyes and pretend you're being strangled to death. "Now go back to your bed and take care of your knee. Time heals all wounds." And he headed back to his library and closed the door.

I sat there for a long time after Dad retreated to the library with the envelope, my good leg cramping under me, staring into the spot in the hall where Andrew John had just recited his debatable poetry. Here, Dad, who really could be quite eloquent when he felt like it, had tried to speak his mind for once, and had met with rejection for it. I struggled back to my feet and went back to my room and sat down. But I couldn't even get started on my solution to poverty again. Almost immediately, I heard another car in the driveway. It was Clarine in a blue Buick, home from the shopping. What Dad called, the Getting and Spending.

For no real reason, I took a walk on my crutch to Cabot's room, even though she was at the country club pool with the others. But if she was home—and as it was turning out, even if she wasn't—I'd definitely go straight to tell her about Dad's envelope. We always kept each other informed about Dad and the various things that happened. These private conversations always took place in her room, because she had a little suite of them, and they were at the remotest end of the back stairs. It would have been the maid's quarters, except Clarine slept in a bigger, nicer room adjoined to mine by a bathroom, more the room of an older sister than a housekeeper. That's because Clarine was more like an older sister than a housekeeper, except of course she was the sister who had to do all the housework. Come to think of it, Clarine was sort of like Cinderella. Except I'd hate to think who that made me and Cabot. Anyway, we called Cabot's room "The Tower."

I went to Cabot's canopy bed and climbed on. If Cabot were there, she'd probably be at her drawing table, sketching a picture. While she was doing it, she'd probably be asking if Dad were rich. Ever since that one Easter drive, she asked it kind of chronically, usually while she was drawing pictures of beautiful models from *Vogue* magazine.

"Who? You mean Dad?"

She'd glance up from her sketchbook. I was being sarcastic.

So once again I'd add it all up for her: the house we lived in, even though it just cost a dollar, the four cars in the garage (three Buicks plus Grandfather's old Dream Machine), the vacations we took, the schools we attended, the sports we played, the company we kept, and arrive at the usual answer. "He better be."

Cabot would shake her head. "I think Grandfather paid for everything. I bet they didn't even buy the dumb Buicks themselves."

"Oh, I think they bought the dumb Buicks themselves."

It was kind of Cabot's job to worry about money. I got everything else. And if she didn't worry with me, I'd do my best to shame her into it.

"Dad named our horses after alcohol," I told her one night. I was trying to sit still, modeling for her. When she didn't even stop drawing for one second when I told her what Dad had done, I said, "Cabot. Heads up. Your horse is an alcoholic."

She frowned and kept drawing. Except eventually she said, "That's not a very nice thing to say about my horse."

"Cutty Sark and Chivas Regal. That's Scotch. Jimmy Beam is bourbon." Jimmybeam was an extra horse. Mother sometimes rode him. "He got his inspiration from the liquor cabinet."

But she was in that denial, I guess. She got rather stubborn about it. "You're so wrong. Their names are just 'Cutty' and 'Chivas.'"

"No, they have last names too. Cutty's last name is Sark, and Chivas's is Regal. Go downstairs and look it up."

"Then what's Jimmybeam's last name?"

"*Beam*. In the cabinet. On the bottle."

"Oh. But just because they might be named that, that doesn't mean they're alcoholics."

"Well, don't you think it's sad Dad names every horse after drinking?"

She sighed. "I wish he'd talk about it." She held up the finished sketch.

Frankly, I couldn't see the resemblance. "That's supposed to be me?"

"You kept moving around."

"I was moving so much I looked like I was wearing that big maroon hat?" We had a portrait of an Elizabethan scholar with a big maroon hat just like it in the library.

Cabot sighed. "I can't draw pictures of real people. I can only draw pictures of *pictures* of real people."

Actually, Cabot was usually very good. But like any kid, the minute you start showing them off, they do something awful. One of her pictures, of a man in yet another big maroon hat, once won a prize in a show at the Cleveland Museum school. When the show was over, Dad hung the picture in the library next to the original man in the big maroon hat. He claimed if he were a collector, he would have chosen Cabot's. Then Cabot said maybe he should pay her like fifty thousand dollars for it. She claimed it wasn't the money, it was the principle. "Did you ever get the money from Dad?"

"Is he rich?"

I think we got pretty repetitive.

One thing that concerned Cabot was Dad's profession: advertising. "Could he really be any good at that? If you don't, like, talk, how can you, like, advertise?"

But we found Dad had found a way. We once went to his library and unlocked his desk and looked through his old portfolio. On each left-hand page was a picture of the ad Dad made up, and on each facing page, a picture of the award he won for it. Cabot went through it, studying the advertisements, and I waited for her to say if they were any good, seeing as she was the artist and all.

It took her forever to finish. Finally I said, "Well? Is he smart, or crazy?"

"Uh, more like smart and lazy."

She turned back to the first ad in the portfolio. "See. This is like, Every picture tells a story."

The ad was for a microchip company. It had the company name in small letters at the bottom. Cabot said that a microchip is a tiny, nondescript little computer that performs a very complicated function once it's placed inside a larger computer. Cabot said Dad's design problem was to make the image of this tiny microchip convey the message that it was performing very high-level computations, therefore replacing some of the best human brains in industry.

She studied the picture and nodded affirmative. "This is smart."

"It's just another gun." I wasn't so thrilled with guns, even pictures of them, I suppose.

"But it's not a gun. It's a gray metal, L-shaped microchip. He had the photo people blow it up so big to make it look like a gun."

Under the gun/microchip, the caption read, "Who killed the boss?"

"Oh, I get it."

She said, "See?"

Then Cabot turned the pages. "Every picture tells a story is a cliché. That's pretty lazy. But he seems to have taken it for all it's worth. Which is pretty smart."

I saw what was happening. As we turned the pages of the portfolio, the more beautiful and original the pictures became, the less willing Dad seemed to use words to explain them. He went from the four-word ad, to the three-word ad, to the two and just the one: the name of the product. And finally, he made a spectacular attempt to eliminate words altogether.

The last picture in the portfolio showed an expressionless man in an impeccable suit sitting at a highly polished mahogany desk floating on top of the Pacific Ocean. Not that we'd ever actually seen it before, but we still recognized this one immediately. After he had returned from the six-week trip to the Coast to work on it, Dad had spontaneously confided at dinner that the whole "shoot" had been a "real nightmare." Mother encouraged him to elaborate. Dad said, Shooting the picture. Making the desk and the model seem as if they were sitting on water. Dragging a float out into the Pacific Ocean. Sinking the float with weights so it wouldn't show in the photograph, but still making it buoyant enough to support the desk, the man, and the chair. Lowering the male model from the helicopter without getting his suit all soaked. And then: waiting for the perfect sunset.

But the finished ad was almost blindingly beautiful. There in the middle of a calm Pacific Ocean, under a hill-size red sunset, sat a dignified man in a perfect suit at an empty, high-gloss desk. The sky was gleaming gold, orange, and yellow. The water was as smooth as a blue mirror. It was a seductive scene, Cabot called it "subliminal beyond belief," and she assured me that anyone who saw the ad was probably dying to buy anything in the picture. That is, if Dad had just bothered to mention what was up for sale. But at the last minute, I guess he refused to mar his masterpiece with words. There was no mention of any product. Not even a logo.

Cabot shook her head. "He went too far. This is *only* a picture tells a story." But, she told me, the client must have calmed down, seeing as Dad won an award for the ad anyway. There was a photograph of him accepting it on the last page in the portfolio.

After that, Dad got promoted to senior senior executive vice president or something, maybe the one sure way to get him to stop creating concepts and driving the clients crazy. Now he could afford to express himself in the purest sense, in utter artistic silence.

• • •

The Tower was over the kitchen, and I could hear Clarine banging pots and pans around downstairs. I could hear Dad too. Laughing. He loved Clarine. They got along well together. I took my crutch and went back to my room and my chair.

But the minute I got there and got started trying to remember how to make everyone rich, just as Grandfather already knew, another car comes screeching up the driveway. I dragged myself to the window. Far below, in the circular part of the driveway, was the beautiful Mickey Knight in her father's hot-wired antique red MG convertible.

It was truly shocking. She was only fourteen, but no matter how hard her father, the brain surgeon, tried to lock up that car, if she really wanted it, she got to it anyway. I watched her jump out and run to our door.

I heard the doorbell peal. I heard Clarine, who preferred Mickey Joslyn to Mickey Knight and didn't make the slightest effort to conceal it, answer the door. I was still at the window, still amazed about the MG, when she burst in my bedroom. And just stood there, blankly looking around. As if she'd never been there before. "Mickey," I said sternly, "you stole your father's car."

She put up her hand. It was wavering weirdly. "Don't even." Her lower lip was quivering.

"I came to make you over!"

She threw herself on the bed, plunged her face in the pillows, and burst into tears.

I got my crutch and hurried over. "Mickey, what happened?!"

"L-L-L-L . . ."

"What? What? Are you saying 'love'?"

She picked up her face and looked at me angrily. "L-L-L . . . ! L-L-L . . . !"

"*Love.*"

Her head rose and fell limply up and down.

"But who, Mickey? Which one?"

"T-t-t-t . . . ," she sobbed.

"Not Thomas."

Her shoulders heaved in assent.

I sat in my armchair and sighed, "But you didn't love him last week."

"I d-d-did so."

No. She didn't. Last week she loved Charles. We'd been at the club, and she'd spent the entire day in the locker room avoiding Thomas, and trying to track Charles down on the phone.

In bits and pieces, which I must say took almost as long as my entire meditation on world hunger, I got the story out of her. She knew *now* that she loved Thomas, but she had found out too late. Just moments ago, he had told her she was self-centered, self-absorbed, self-serving, and selfish. He'd called her "almost a man."

"But, Mickey," I said gently, "maybe you only think you love Thomas because he doesn't love you."

It was the right idea but the wrong way to put it. She went from shallow hysteria into deep hysteria, charting whole new waters in the expression of devastation and grief. Her face turned pink with clover-shaped patches, her neck turned blue, and her hands blanched from red to white. I debated whether to call her father. Maybe he had some kind of miracle drug that could restore his daughter to her lovable, selfish self. As it stood, Mickey Knight was totally humbled, and I didn't think it was good for her health.

Clarine knocked on the door and opened it. "That's enough,"

she said, staring with distaste at the broken-down spectacle that once was the perfectly self-possessed Mickey Knight.

I took my crutch and led Clarine out of the room. "Clarine, what should we do, she's *heartbroken.*"

"Gotta have one to bust one," Clarine said, chuckling at her own little joke.

"*Clarine.*" I loved Clarine, but I hated the way she loved to hate Mickey Knight.

"Well, which one is it anyway? Matt's friend Charles, Christopher Bridges, or the *nice* boy, *Thomas?*"

Mickey wailed from the bedroom.

"Clarine!" I cried. "Hush up!"

"Your knee is not so hurt I can't wash your mouth out anymore."

I remembered that old tough love routine of hers, and apologized.

"Well, she doesn't look so good," said Clarine, sulking a little. "I've a mind to call her family."

"You do that and things will start to die!" That was Mickey Knight, from the bedroom.

I hopped back in and closed the door. "Mickey? Are you okay?"

She was sitting up in bed, brushing her hair. She looked beautiful again, like one of those movie stars who sits up in bed, brushing her hair. "I'm fine. But I don't understand why your mother doesn't deep-six that maid."

"*Mickey.*" I loved Mickey, but I hated the way she loved to hate Clarine.

Then I got the whole story out of her. Thomas had told her he was now in love with someone else, a beautiful, sweet girl who was all woman. When the girl turned sixteen he was going to fuck her and marry her, but not in that order.

"Did he really say that, Mickey? Did he use that word?"

"Oh, Boyce, don't be so naive. Of course not. He's a gentleman." A little leftover sob escaped from her after that.

Mickey had pressed Thomas for the name of the girl. Though at first he refused to disclose it, in the end he blurted it out. Naturally, it was Jo, the other Mickey.

"Does Jo know about this?" I was thinking, you know. Canadian tennis. How that wretched game was going to ruin the neighborhood.

"Yeah. She's home, thinking about it. But I didn't kill Jo. It's him I want to die."

I didn't blame her for not killing Jo.

"But you know what?" she said, putting the finishing touches on her hair. "I'm going to get him back?"

She would, too. Every boy dumped Mickey for Jo. Just not for long.

"I mean, fear not."

After Mickey's amazing recovery from her alarming emotional breakdown, she said maybe she should rest before trying to make me over. So we sat around talking, for hours.

By late afternoon, assorted Buicks and visiting cars were doing their standard Saturday comings and goings up and down the driveway. Dusk fell. Down past the long front lawn, the lights came up with the low lamps, cozily leading the way to the house. Mother and Dad ducked their heads in to say good-bye, on their way to a party. Matt came by and said "Hi." He took one trip around my room, with one eye on Mickey Knight the whole time, and left. Clarine came, and, as if she were feeding something evil in a cage, cautiously slid a tray of sandwiches in along the floor, then quickly closed the door. Lucy, then Luke, came to dutifully kiss me good night. The only one who didn't stop by was Cabot.

. . .

It was an almost heroic feat, to sustain a dialogue as long as we did. We punctuated, or accented, it by going from the bed to the vanity table to apply Mickey's makeup. Leaning shoulder to shoulder at the mirror, the mascara, lipstick, and eyeliner became our alternate tools of expression; our heightened color, blackened eyes, reddened lips, visible evidence of the depth of our search for meaning. And we hadn't even gotten past the neighborhood boys.

Then, out of the blue, Mickey asked me, "Hey, what did you do all day anyway, with that cast on your leg? I'd kill myself if I had to just sit in a chair."

"Me? Nothing." It reminded me of my injury though, and how my knee hurt, and I rubbed off all the makeup and took my crutch and went to my bed. "I sat here too." I meant, not just in a chair.

"See? I'd die. You sat on a bed and a chair."

I shrugged, "It's not so bad. You can read a book. You can write a letter."

Mickey brightened. "You wrote a letter? Who to? A love letter?"

I didn't really know what to call it, so I didn't answer. You know, you don't want to lie. But my silence made her suspicious.

"It better not be to Thomas."

I shook my head it wasn't, but it just made her more curious.

"Really. Who'd you write it to? Was it Thomas? It was, wasn't it?"

"No."

"You did so! You wrote it to Thomas!"

"I wrote it to my grandfather!"

Mickey blinked at me in the mirror. "But. But I thought both your grandfathers are dead."

"Well, they are."

"Then . . . then how did you write them a letter?"

"In my head. I just wrote it in my head."

"But . . ."

I wasn't too crazy to explain it to her further. But she was kind of waiting to hear it, you could tell. She was staring at me pretty hard in the mirror. I said, "Relax, I just wrote it in my head."

She still just stood there staring at me, though. But eventually she asked, "Well, then which one did you write it to?"

"My father's father."

"The one who gave you this house for a dollar?"

I nodded. "I really liked him. Besides, I owed him a thank-you note." I was wearing the pearls, and took them out from under my tee shirt to show her. Of course, I had already told her all about them on the phone.

Mickey nodded they were nice, and went back to applying makeup. But after that, she kind of kept one eye fixed on me through the mirror.

Then I remembered what else I'd done today. I felt so close to Mickey by now, what with all the talking we'd done, I thought I could say anything. Even ideas that were all messed up and just half formed. "I also thought about what to do about poor people."

Mascara wand stopped midair, Mickey said, "Who? Who's poor?"

"Poor *people*. They're everywhere. I almost fixed the problem though." I grinned at her via the mirror. "I thought so long and hard about it, I almost gave the whole world a makeover."

She carefully closed the mascara wand, not to clump it. "That sounds like fun."

"I'm not kidding. I actually solved world poverty. But then the doorbell rang and the mailman came. And now I have to start all over again."

"Oh boy." She opened the mascara wand again. I guess she'd decided to start that all over again.

"The thing I think about poverty is, I'm not so sure it should be, like, acceptable. You know what I mean?"

But then, having said that much, I couldn't even begin to remember my original solution to the problem. I began to feel that the idea I'd had about making everyone rich now might elude me forever. I began to blame it on the post office. I began to wonder how many brilliant solutions to global problems had been lost because of the post office. Because the world is full of mail trucks screeching up driveways, doorbells piercing into the void, men in blue suits delivering bad news, wrecking your hopes and dreams, ruining everything.

"I mean, Mickey, nothing's black and white, right? So why does poverty always win?"

No, that wasn't what I was trying to say either, not at all. I was never going to remember the solution now. But then I thought I had better. I'd just have to go back to the very beginning.

So I began to tell Mickey what I'd seen downtown on the Easter drive with Dad. I told of the little children with the dirty faces and the houses without doors and the old people sitting on cement steps because they didn't have any chairs. I told of the woman who had tried to get dressed up for Easter with her hat, but then sat down on the sidewalk when she didn't have shoes.

Then I went even further, recounting pictures I'd seen in *Time* magazine, of an African country where the people were starving. And in *Life*, a picture of a tiny Mexican Indian boy standing next to a tall American girl, whom the story said was the same age as the boy, only the boy's growth had been stunted because half the year there was no rain where he lived, and nothing grew to eat.

And then I have to admit I went on a total roll, on and on, recounting for Mickey every image of abject poverty I could remember, until I was nearly pleading with her that it had to be stopped, and since nobody else had done it, it was up to us for sure.

• • •

When I looked to Mickey, I was surprised she wasn't working on herself anymore. She was staring at me through the mirror with her mouth all puckered, a tube of red lipstick poised in hand. She had so many coats on already, her lips weren't even close to red. Like old roses, they were almost black. "Mickey? What color is that?"

She glanced at the label on the bottom. "Chanel. Fatal Red."

"You better stop. It's too dark. You'll look dead."

She dropped the tube in her makeup kit. "So does this poverty thing mean you don't want me to make you over?"

"Oh. No, but, see, I have this theory, but I just can't remember what it is. It's designed to make everyone rich. If it works, just imagine."

"Well," she said, "then maybe you should think about it some more. Jo's home thinking. You're here thinking. You guys are unbelievable. But go. Go ahead. Think."

I shrugged and took her advice. I lay there for a while, very still. It was the first time there had been silence between us all day, but I figured it was for a higher purpose and all. But no matter what I did or how hard I tried, I couldn't remember how to make everyone rich. Mickey was patient, she didn't say anything. I mean all she said was "You know, pearls don't really go with a tee shirt."

But you wouldn't believe it. Something when she said that. I suddenly sat up, feeling lucky. "Hey, Mick? You know the death wish?"

Mickey grabbed her eyelash curler, and applied the metal instrument to her right eye, the left glued to me through the mirror.

"Well, the death wish is this thing that everyone has, that they wish they could die. But just to see what it's like. But, it's just curiosity. But my question is, if everybody has a death wish because they're curious, how do we know everybody isn't dying . . . of curiosity?"

She had begun with an eyebrow brush in furious strokes, so I excused her from answering.

"So listen. What if the most uncurious person in the world comes along? I mean they're very curious on the one hand, but not at all on the other. They're curious only about *life*. And it's a woman. And she's a teacher, and she starts a school, called a Lack of Curiosity School, to teach how not to have the death wish. And she teaches all the little children. She channels and guides all their little curiosity. She totally fills them up with it, but only on the one hand, see, and not on the other. Because of her, there is no space left in the children's minds for the death wish. Then maybe a whole generation would grow up without the death wish, and maybe, if it worked, nobody would ever die!"

I lay back down to think it through. "But that's probably unrealistic. Because everyone has to die."

I rolled back over and looked at Mickey. She was vigorously removing makeup with a huge wad of cotton balls.

"But," I continued, "that's just the theory. Like in science class, we simply extract the method. We invent schools just like the lack of curiosity schools, but not to end death, to end *poverty*."

She winged the whole wet wad of cotton balls into my brass wastebasket. It sounded like a gun.

"People have to die, but they don't have to be poor."

Now she was clawing at the lid to a fat, flat jar, then banging it on the edge of the vanity table, then slamming it with the handle of my antique silver brush. I was about to ask if she'd like me to try, when, with a grunt, she finally got it open.

She began to smear clay masque all over her face.

"And at these new Lack of Curiosity Schools we invent? Just

like we could have done with the death wish if everybody didn't have to die, we just eradicate the thought of poverty from the children's minds, and replace it with the thought of wealth. The words poverty and hunger no longer exist. There is no way to say to them. There is no way to *think* them. Then there could never be a hungry person in this world, because poverty and hunger would have become *unthinkable!*"

There. I blinked up at the ceiling, to see if that was finally it.

But no, it wasn't. Not the brilliant solution I had arrived at earlier. That, the real solution, perhaps it was gone forever. But I had thought of it. I know I had. But the mailman. I shook my head and closed my eyes, idly playing with my pearls, rudely forgetting my friend at the mirror.

When I came to, she was hanging over me. She had covered her whole face, except for her black lips and one black eyebrow, with the wet clay masque and she was as gray as a ghost. But her eyes. Was it fear? Yes, plus it was fury, like to the hundredth power. "Mickey," I whispered, stunned at the transformation. She didn't look like an After anymore. She looked worse than the worst Before. "What *happened?*"

"Lack of Curiosity Schools?" she said, the one eyebrow twitching wildly, cracking the forehead of her masque.

I didn't dare defend them. They had really ticked her off.

"So far we've got you on crutches, writing a letter to your dead grandparent, and doing something I can't even explain to poor people. Are you on painkillers?"

I couldn't even answer, because it was riveting, fascinating, what was happening to Mickey's face as the masque on it dried. Her eyelids began to droop, her lips began to curl, her right eyebrow arched up, and then her whole face fixed, like a photograph just done developing. And then, I don't know, she seemed set, as in for life.

She said one last thing, though, before that happened. "Would you do me a favor. Boyce?"

I nodded.

"Would you stop talking about poor people?"

I nodded.

"And can I give you a little advice?"

I closed my eyes. I couldn't even look at the masque anymore.

"This is *not* the way to get made over."

Soon after Mickey Knight went peeling down the driveway in the re-hot-wired red MG, I took my crutch and went to Cabot's room and poked her with it and woke her up. That is, I didn't exactly wake her, because I could see her eyes were half-open beneath her blond hair, which always looked perfectly brushed, even when she was lying in bed under her canopy. Now it was spilled all over the pillow, shimmering like anything in the moonlight from the window. "Sis," I said. "Wake up."

"I am up. Did that friend of yours leave?"

"Guess what?"

"Did she drive herself home?"

I wrapped my free arm around the post at the end of the bed. "Dad got an envelope back in the mail."

"Oh. How come her parents let her have that car? She's only fourteen years old."

"It's hot-wired. They're always away."

"She looks about forty though. I mean, what do you say all day to a forty-year-old?"

"Are you going to listen?"

"You won't tell me? Oh, I guess I'm not as cool."

I almost said she was too cool, but caught myself in time. You start telling your sister she's cool, and she immediately starts thinking she's cooler than you are. "Listen, Dad wrote a story or something, and it got rejected."

Cabot sat up, instantly forgiving me for Mickey Knight. "Wow."

"Andrew John the mailman brought it back. And he writes stuff too. And he gets rejected. He's a poet or something. You should have heard him in the hall."

Cabot said, "Well, I think Dad's smart."

I said, "Well, I think he's smarter than Andrew John."

I hopped closer with my crutch and sat on the edge of the bed. "Cabbie? Do you think it's possible to end poverty once and for all?"

She looked at me wide-eyed, as if I'd frightened her.

"Don't be scared. Just yes or no."

She hugged her knees to her chin, forming a white mountain out of her eiderdown. "I'm not sure, but maybe. But I don't think so. Not completely. No."

"Okay. So if you knew that in your heart, you'd never mention it, right?"

"Uh, I guess so."

"See. That's like Dad."

Her face tightened up with the effort of concentration. "But I don't get it, though."

"People who don't talk much . . . maybe they do it because of injustices or something. Because you really can't do anything about injustices. A smart person like Dad knows it's better just to keep your mouth shut."

"Really?" She started thinking about it, rocking back and forth.

"Yes. In his heart, he knows it doesn't make a difference what anyone says. Remember? Every *picture* tells a story. Maybe the story doesn't tell the story."

Cabot asked uncertainly, "But what's that got to do with poverty? And Andrew John bringing that envelope back?"

I said, *"See?"* But the truth is, I didn't have a clue anymore. I was tired, I was injured, I had thought all day long beyond my abilities and I now I couldn't remember any of it anymore. What I might have said was that there are some things that were never intended to be expressed. Certain visions, dreams, flashes of understanding, the fleeting hold we sometimes have on knowledge or compassion, are simply not transferable. But I didn't know how to say that, and realized now it was useless to try.

Cabot fell back on her pillows, staring sadly up at her huge canopy, which Dad liked to call the other roof over her head. I reached for my crutch, feeling sorry that all day long, I had more or less promised something I hadn't been able to deliver. Cabot watched me get to my feet. "So you think that explains everything? Dad included?"

She was really trying to understand it, you could tell. But for sure, neither of us knew what we were talking about anymore. "Definitely."

"Does *she* have anything to do with this?"

"Who?" I asked innocently.

"Your old friend."

"Of course not."

"In that case, I'll think about it."

"No. Don't."

Her head rose from the pillow. *"Don't?* What is this?"

"It'll only hurt you in the end. It's hopeless."

She sat full up, in protest. "Hey, it's not hopeless. It's just hard." Then she fell back down.

Hard. It was just a kind word, but I was awfully happy to hear it anyway.

I started for the door. "Well, good night, sis." I liked calling her "sis," don't ask me why. "I have to go finish a letter now."

I turned and stood in her door a second. She looked so nice

lying there, I heard myself saying, "You know, you look a lot like the princess and the pea."

"Oh. Thank you, if that's good."

"It's good. It's very good."

"I guess it depends whether it's the princess, or the pea."

"The princess wouldn't have been anything without the pea. But you look more like the princess." I left her little suite of rooms and limped sleepily down the hall. Then I heard her call "Zu!" and turned around.

I leaned against her doorway.

She was sitting up again, all awake again. "Just so you know. Now that I'm a princess, I think I've changed my mind. I think you could end it, if you really were a princess, and were really rich, and very kind."

Knowing what I had only briefly known of hope, and would never again attempt to convey, a congenial silence like Dad's seemed the only generous response. So in keeping with that, I murmured, but strictly to myself, "Good night, sweet princess."

THIRTEEN

I never really asked her if she lost her job or resigned it, but on Fridays by now, Cabot too was always early for school. So we often ran across each other in the empty halls. Cabot also went to the Academy, but she was one year behind.

Anyway, one Friday, "Hi, sis," I said.

"Hi, Zuzu."

Nothing to write home about. We both walked on. But a moment later, the girl who had been sitting ahead of me in Assembly since we were four-year-olds in preschool came up behind me at my locker. "Boyce?" she said, very softly, as if being careful not to make me shy like a horse would if you came up too quick from behind.

I still shied anyway. I knew who it was, and I whirled around. "Yes, Mary Parker?"

There were several reasons to fear this girl. She was brilliant, and her father was a bus driver. She was the smartest, the poorest, and probably the coolest girl in school. Actually, she was too cool for school. Except she didn't get credit for it, because her father was this bus driver.

"Oh," she said, "nothing."

"Oh," I said, "okay. Cool."

She was going to go now. Then her famous curiosity got the

better of her. "But why did your sister just call you that name?"

She quickly looked both ways down the empty hall, as if she were already sorry she'd brought the whole thing up, and was going to go now. We had sometimes talked in class, but we had never, in ten whole years, talked like this in the hall. "But if you don't want to tell me, I'll just . . . leave."

Not at all. Mary Parker, school genius, had just asked me a question I knew I could answer. "It's my name. I mean, my nick-name, I guess."

She brightened up a little. "Z-u-z-u, right? I can't think of an alternate spelling."

The truth of it is, I didn't know. But I wasn't about to tell the school genius I couldn't spell my own name. "I guess my father thought the whole thing up."

"Did he say where he got it, though? I just want to make sure."

"Uh, I think from some movie?"

Her face broke into a smile, which didn't happen to this partic-ular girl all that often. "I had a feeling when I heard it."

Then she kind of packed up, moving her books from one arm to the other like she was getting all packed and ready to go. Instead of good-bye or see ya, or actually just going though, she added, "Not a bad namesake for you."

It was kind of understood, once I agreed this was so, she would go. All I had to do was just nod confidently and it was over. But I couldn't, see, because I had no idea who this Zuzu person my father nicknamed me after even was. Now I felt really dumb for never asking my father. Like I had the intellectual curiosity of a dormouse, whatever that was.

Mary Parker said, "Zuzu was Jimmy Stewart's little girl in *It's a Wonderful Life*. I mean, that's the reference, right?" But she already knew I had no idea what she was talking about.

I nodded confidently. I thought she would go.

"I sure hope what happened to her father doesn't happen to yours."

"What happened to hers again?" But I was thinking, Come on, what so tragic could have happened to a man in a movie called *It's a Wonderful Life*.

Mary Parker studied me, her eyes like arches within arches, her thin brown brows raised, an expression that gave you the feeling she had just made a rather earthshaking scientific discovery about you, but was taking it all in stride. When we were little girls in lower school, she'd once turned around and asked me if I didn't find the size of our desks "somewhat ironic." And didn't I agree that the school should have either smaller desks or bigger teachers? With the same detached concern, she now asked, "You mean you've never seen the movie?"

"I must have missed it."

Mary Parker blinked. "But it's a classic. It's on every Christmas. Like ten times every Christmas. You missed it a lot. But you know the story, right?"

"Is Santa Claus in it?"

"Okay, the protagonist, George Bailey, played by Jimmy Stewart? The actor?"

It was a little annoying, her having to point that out, that the guy playing the part was an actor. "Yeah?"

"Well, he gives up on his dream of leaving this small town he lives in and he gets married and has a lot of kids and takes over the building-and-loan association but then he loses everybody's money and then he tries to kill himself."

"That's a wonderful *life*?"

She shrugged. "It has a happy ending."

"Like, how happy?"

Mary Parker looked up the hallway. "You know. All happy endings are alike. Just like happy families."

No, I didn't know that. I looked up the hallway with her, but in the opposite way. People were arriving for school. Mickey Knight was coming in the door with the club; Jo came right behind with another. Jo was so beautiful, she got her own club. I glanced sideways at Mary Parker. "So the guy doesn't die?"

"George Bailey? No way."

I didn't tell her that "George" was my father's name too. But I was already planning on telling Cabot. This was a new development.

"Anyway, your father must know movies, to nickname you after Zuzu. Zuzu was quite a character."

"Was she smart?"

Mary Parker winced. "Well, she was young."

"I see."

"Actually, she wasn't that bright at all, for a three-year-old. She had this single red rose she got, and when the bloom drooped on the stem, she wanted her father to Scotch tape it back together. Like then it would live. Pretty pathetic, actually."

"She got a single red rose?"

"The point is, Zuzu was sort of a moron. But let's just call her a little loser."

All right already. I started moving books around on the shelf of my locker. The two clubs passed by, but they didn't pick me up today because I was busy talking to Mary Parker. I was kind of ticked off at my father, to nickname me after some three-year-old moron in a movie. I was beginning to wish I had Mary Parker's father. He sounded like a smart guy, just naming her "Mary." Then she turns out to be this genius and all.

The clubs turned and went into class. Mary Parker was still there at my locker. I was still moving my books around, like it was rather important that they be moved around today, and not only today, but right now, immediately, and without further delay. I kept wishing I could ask Mary Parker a few things about her father. But I couldn't even think of asking Mary Parker about her father, seeing as her father was this bus driver. "You going in?" I asked instead, real casual, clicking my locker shut.

"Well, I was thinking of having a smoke."

A smoke? I looked around. "Here?"

She jerked her head, meaning, Outside, jerk. "Want to come? I'll teach you how to light them."

"I know how to light matches," I said, somewhat offended by now. I thought Mary Parker thought I was such a moron slash little loser I didn't know how to light matches. Here I had kind of done her this favor by asking her to walk into class with me, as probably no one in school had ever done before, and this was the thanks I got. I was somewhat offended.

"Bet you can't with one hand."

Oh. With one hand. That was different.

"You ride horses, don't you? I heard you're pretty good."

"Oh. Thanks."

"Well, say you want a smoke while you're riding your horse. For your own safety, you should know how to light up with one hand. Like the cowboys do."

I mean, this is not why I call Mary Parker a genius. But then she huddled close to my locker and showed me how, using a pencil and a pack of matches, saying if you do it right, you don't get badly burned.

I said, "Cool."

The bell rang. Mary Parker glanced at the Assembly door. "Anyway. I'll go in with you. Sure."

So for the first time ever, we walked into Assembly together. We took our seats alphabetically, me behind her as always, which was just one of those accidents of birth.

• • •

I guess it was because of that cowboy thing that, after ten whole years, I decided to take a chance on Mary Parker. So later that day, during afternoon Assembly, I passed up a note asking if she wanted to do something together out of school.

This was taking a chance, because, if you didn't notice before, doing something with Mary Parker out of school just wasn't something that was ever done. The other girls claimed she was simply too smart for the rest of us, but probably the truth of it was she was simply too poor. Other kids took ski trips together, or met at the club in summer and signed out golf carts at the pro shop and rode across the back nine over to someone's house so we could hang out there until the pro shop would close. And sometimes we even golfed, or played tennis, or had swim meets at the pool. But Mary Parker went home every day at three, never was seen on a Saturday, and all summer, just disappeared.

She sent the note right back. I figured this meant, Return to Sender or, at best, Address Correction Requested, and so I thought that that was a pretty dumb chance I took, and I slipped the note into my book, planning to keep it for life, but only as a reminder not to take dumb chances anymore. But later that hour I opened my book and glanced at the note anyway. Mary Parker had scribbled, *A movie. Downtown.* I wasn't allowed to go downtown, but I still wrote back, *Sure.* She wrote back, *Then I'll teach you how to knock off a store.*

I was to meet her on the last car of the Rapid Transit at around noon.

All that Saturday morning I lurked in my room. Cars began whizzing up and down the driveway. Mother left for golfing in her Buick. Clarine left for Getting and Spending in her Buick, but came home all too soon. Mr. Carter, Dad's friend who played the saxophone, arrived in his old Ford. Once they got started, once the music was filling the house up, I slipped down the back stairs and ran out the sunroom door, calling to anyone who could hear me over the music I'd be at the movies. You had to say where you were going. Nobody had ever said it had to be heard.

At the platform, I stood leaning out, watching for the white head-lamps in the taxi-colored train.

The plan was that I would dial Mary Parker's number from the Shaker Boulevard stop as soon as I saw the Rapid, and by the time the train arrived at the edge of Cleveland near Mary's house, she'd be waiting by the tracks. I saw the first car poke through the mist, hurriedly dialed and hung up, and ran down the long wooden stairs.

Dropping my fare into the box, I remembered loving the Rapid, back when it cost less than fifty cents. To us, a ride on the Rapid was the only alternative to a ride on the roller coasters Mother had banned, and we used to beg Dad to let us do it. Even though he was partial to blue Buicks as his means of trans-portation, he'd sometimes take us on the train, take us off at Shaker Square, buy us toys at FAO Schwarz, call a car to take us home. But the train seemed newer then. Now it seemed clank-ing and slow, and seemed to labor under the weight of unful-filled promise, like, say, if The Little Engine That Could never had.

Three boys sat ahead of me, blond kids in Cleveland Indians caps wearing baseball mitts. I felt like asking them if they were on their way to sit in the bleachers at a game. My brother Luke, who was always telling me things I didn't necessarily need to hear about professional sports, had assured me the thing to do was call the

Cleveland Indians "The Tribe," and now I felt like pretending I knew a lot about baseball, and asking the three kids if they were going to see The Tribe this afternoon, or what they thought of The Tribe this year, and what did they think about the old pitching on The Tribe. I just felt like letting them know I knew the Cleveland Indians were called The Tribe, don't ask me why. I bet because they were boys.

But I eavesdropped first, to see if they even knew the Cleveland Indians were called The Tribe. They weren't talking about baseball, though. One of the boys was telling about something he'd seen when riding in a car one evening with his dad. A green pickup truck with a big dog on its roof. But when his dad pulled alongside the pickup, it turned out that the dog wasn't a real dog, but a huge cardboard sign in the shape of dog. An advertising dog.

"I really wanted it to be real," the kid kept saying, over and over, switching his baseball cap so the visor was first in the front, then in the back, getting so worked up about it I felt sorry myself the dog was a fraud.

The other two boys felt sorry too. One of them said, "Maybe it was real and you just thought it was cardboard, just like when you thought it was real, it was really cardboard."

The three of them were making plans to go play on the highway and look for the green truck with the fake dog when I gave up on my plans about The Tribe and started looking out the window for Mary Parker.

As the trained slowed up, I saw her waiting on the platform. It was the first time I'd ever seen her out of uniform. She was dressed all in black. Black, boys' clothes. Boys' black high-top sneakers. Big black baggy pants. Long black turtleneck. Mary Parker looked cool. She walked unhurriedly, if not reluctantly, toward me and the last car.

I looked down at myself. Just as I had suspected after I'd already left the house and couldn't go back, I should have worn something else. I was dressed too clean and too like I was going for a ride. Not like a ride on the Rapid, a ride like on a horse. I had old jeans, which was fine, but my black jacket and my good boots Mother had brought home from a Parisian riding apparel store, and they were kind of crisp and polished, which looks good on a horse but this was the Rapid, and I had the feeling Mary Parker might think I didn't know how to ride the Rapid right.

The train stopped and she got on. I gave her a lamo high sign, and she started slowly toward me down the aisle.

The Rapid Transit ran aboveground all the way to downtown, then gained speed and hurtled under Terminal Tower, the main station in Cleveland. It took about half an hour. Except some half hours seem longer than others. Everything I might have normally just blurted out didn't sound all that smart in my head, so then I started trying to sound smart in my head, and that slowed everything down.

But then after the three kids in the Cleveland Indians caps got off, I gave up on sounding smart and told Mary Parker about the green pickup and the advertising dog, the news of which she received thoughtfully. I told her the Cleveland Indians were called The Tribe, as I wasn't sure whether the stuff Luke knew was the type of thing a genius would know, or what. She just nodded her head again though. Finally, I said, "We're just going to the movies, right?" I was a little worried about that reference she'd made in her note to robbing a store.

Mary Parker said, "Yeah. To the movies."

Other than that, we rode in silence most of the way.

At Terminal Tower I told Mary Parker she should choose the movie, because I figured she was the genius and all. I mean I didn't say that, naturally, I just figured it is all. But then when we bought *The Plain Dealer* at the newsstand, the movie she picked was a double feature called *Curse of the Werewolf* and *Shadow of the Cat*.

She looked up from the paper. "You're not scared, are you?"

"No, I'm not scared of a movie." So after I said that, then it was obviously too late to back down.

"Fear is the opposite of love," Mary Parker said, folding the newspaper and placing it on a wooden bench directly next to the pale hand of a little old man in a worn overcoat.

I turned my head to nod at her for more.

"And love is only knowledge."

I was still trying to figure it out as we went into the basement of Higbee's and bought a chocolate Frosty, then went up on the escalator in Terminal Tower and came out into Public Square.

The movies didn't start until three o'clock, so we had a couple of hours to kill. Mary Parker said she'd give me a tour of downtown. "I've been here," I said. "A lot." I hadn't, not a lot, really not much at all, even including Easter Sundays, but I said it anyway, don't ask me why.

"Have you seen the lake?"

"Seen it. I've sailed on it."

"Oh."

I hated when I said it, though. I hate it when people say they've sailed on a lake when all they were asked was if they'd seen it before. After that, I decided not to talk for a while.

We walked toward Fred's Fish Market on the pier, where Dad had done the high-speed drive-by that Easter I was talking about before. I thought as we walked that nobody in the cars going by would know I was walking around town with a genius. The only reason I even knew was because Mrs. Closky had once sent Mary

Parker down the hall on a bogus errand to get her out of the room. Then Mrs. Closky told us Mary Parker would be classes ahead of students such as ourselves, except the school genius so often skipped school. It was one of those morality tales, I guess, except all it really taught us was that the teachers were mad that they bored Mary Parker to tears.

"Were you born here?" she asked me.

"No, in New York."

"Oh. I was born here."

"My dad was born here," I told her.

"Mine too."

I thought maybe now Mary Parker would say something about her father, the bus driver, and maybe even explain how she got so brilliant, like which side of the family did the geniuses come from and was her father a brilliant bus driver and so on. But she didn't say anything like that, and I didn't ask.

We crossed the highway and started walking up the long wooden pier. The restaurant at the end was closed. We looked in the windows. There were captain's chairs turned upside down on round wooden tables, and bare wooden floors. It didn't look like the type of place I would want to eat in, but I didn't say so, because I was afraid that maybe Mr. Parker had once taken Mary Parker to dinner here.

Out past the restaurant, thick wooden dock posts marked the end of the pier. Mary Parker and I each held on to one and leaned out over the water. Far below, the lake looked as if it had been bombed. The water was bleak with muck, odd pieces of driftwood, or just wood, or just garbage, floated around. About a hundred yards out to the left, a rusted old barge lay swamped like a beached iron whale. "They don't call it 'Erie' for nothing," she said.

Even so, after standing there a while, I began to like the way it looked. It was so bleak and forlorn, it was almost beautiful. Out by the horizon, the gray of the water merged with the sky, making the desolation complete. I began to think it was good that something so weak in its individual parts could impress you so powerfully as a whole. All told, it was some strange lake. Of course, what did you expect from a body of water that was famous for tributaries that burned?

We both hung there on our dock posts, sometimes shaking our heads, as if the sight of the Great Lake was unspeakably sad. Then, when the feeling was over, we both turned at the same time and walked in silence back up the pier.

We went by Public Square again, and I wondered where the Half Shell was, a concert stage that was sometimes used for choirs at Christmas. "I sang a solo here with the Glee Club when I was little," I found myself telling Mary Parker. "The piano lady chose me because she said I looked like a choirboy. My mother tried to put a red bow in my hair so I'd look like a girl, but she couldn't get it to stick. So I guess everybody thought I was a boy when I sang."

I remembered how frightened and cold I'd been when I stepped forward to sing a Christmas carol alone in front of the hundreds of people in Public Square. But then I had seen my father in the gray felt hat in the first row, and I wasn't so cold and afraid anymore.

"You still look like a choirboy."

I didn't mind the truth, coming from her.

We crossed Euclid Avenue. It was one of the first cold days of September, and there weren't many people around. Since now there were so many shopping malls in the suburbs, I guess it didn't make sense to go downtown just to buy stuff anymore. I could still remember trips here with my mother, getting black patent leather shoes and flared wool coats in a blue like the Buicks, and maybe a velvet dress in dark green with a white pique collar. At the big department stores, Halles and Higbee's, there was Santa Claus at Christmas, and escalators made with brown wood slats that your mom's high heel could get caught in if you didn't pull on her hand and warn her from experience before she got on, and lots of red wall-to-wall carpeting, and nice older women with glasses dangling from their necks on little thin ropes, and men too, who carefully wrote down with pencils where to send our packages, and repaid us for our patience with hard candy. And from the women, sometimes, soft, strange-feeling kisses.

Passing these stores made me feel old.

"Want to rob Woolworth's?"

Mary Parker had stopped in front of the five-and-dime store.

"Uh. Not really."

"No?"

"I don't think so."

"Ever been in Woolworth's?"

"Uh. Not really."

"Well, here's your big chance."

The old wooden floorboards knocked loudly under my riding boots as I followed Mary in her silent black high-tops toward a section in the back. "What are we doing?" I whispered. "I'm not allowed to rob stores."

I guess she didn't hear me though.

At a counter under a sign that said NOTIONS was a wide woman with a tall, white, beehive hairdo. Mary Parker stopped and stared at her, and I stood behind. "Mary," I whispered, "what are notions?"

"What do you think?"

"Ideas?"

"Yeah. Bad ones. Look around."

Mary Parker started walking slowly up and down the aisles, lightly touching the items on the displays. She toyed with a package of one-inch elastic, ran her finger around the circle of a wooden embroidery hoop, fondled a pair of what were called dress shields and passed them all by. Then she stopped at the hair accessories. She reached for a card of bobby pins, deftly folding the edge of it down. Then she passed behind me and said, "Take those."

"No thanks."

"Just do it. Don't be so scared."

I stood there and watched Mary Parker head for the counter and the clerk with the white beehive under the NOTIONS sign. And I looked back at the bobby pins.

I couldn't think of one reason to take them. I didn't want them. Bobby pins wouldn't even stay in my hair. I could take them for Cabot, the one with the pretty long hair. But Cabot would get confused if I just came home and said, "Here, I brought you some bobby pins." She'd say, "You brought me some bobby pins?" And I couldn't explain it by saying they were hot bobby pins, and therefore far more collectible.

Even so, I began to consider stealing them. I looked over at Mary Parker, who was now ordering black ribbon from the clerk with the white beehive under the NOTIONS sign. I looked back at the bobby pins. They were arranged on the card in four separate fans, and a girl with a bouffant hairdo whom I had no desire to look like smiled out at me from the corner. I scowled back at her, stroking what there was of my hair. I stood there so long that that girl on the card and I entered into a kind of staring contest. Except then maybe I realized. Maybe she wasn't staring at me at all. Maybe she was trying to tell me something. Save me. *Fear is the opposite of love*.

I looked toward Mary Parker. The clerk with the white bee-hive had gone to cut the black ribbon, and Mary Parker quickly waved at me, palm up. I scanned up and down my aisle. Nobody was there. So I grabbed the card with the bobby pin girl and shoved it in my jacket pocket. About one second later, I heard the clerk with the white beehive bellow an obscenity I won't even mention at Mary Parker. I threw the bobby pin girl into a bin of chiffon scarves and ran for the door, my boots clattering along the floorboards, Mary Parker's sneakers slapping fast behind.

Outside, we didn't stop running until we'd rounded three corners. Then Mary Parker emptied her pockets. She had a yard of black grosgrain ribbon, a bright pink polyester chiffon scarf, a spool of cream-colored cotton thread. She reached under her shirt and pulled the last item out. It was the card with the bobby pin girl. "Isn't this yours?"

I grinned. I was weirdly glad to see her. But when I reached, Mary Parker pulled her away like I didn't deserve her and put the card in her pocket. "Come on. Let's bring this stuff back."

Oh. "But we'll be returning to the scene of the crime."

"I know," she said, somewhat exasperated. "That's the whole point."

"Right." Sometimes, I swear, I have no idea what I'm talking about.

So we went back over to Woolworth's, opened the side door, took a few steps in and dumped everything, then turned and high-tailed it for the second time out of the store.

Don't ask me why, but when we finally stopped running, and laughing, to me, personally, the whole thing started to make a whole lot of sense. Maybe crime's not the best way to build up your confidence, win friends, and influence people, but it worked for me, because then I knew Mary Parker was my friend, and once I knew that, I really didn't even mind going to jail.

We walked several blocks toward the theater, past the Union Club, a noble old, grimy building, where Grandfather used to take us on winter Saturdays so we could roll white cue balls around the billiards tables and drink fake cocktails at the bar. When Mary Parker stopped to look at the building, I just stood there looking along with her. This time I didn't say things like I'd been inside, that we belonged.

"Don't look now," she said as we walked on, "but there's a psychopath behind us."

Mary Parker turned to look, though. She took her sweet time, too. "Sorry. He's not a psychopath," she said, turning back around. "I think he's a sociopath."

"We're going pretty slow."

"Don't freak out. See if he follows us to the movie."

At the ticket window, I finally turned around. But there was only a nice-looking businessman in a hat. "Where?"

"Uh, the only guy there?"

It was the nice-looking businessman in the hat. He was standing beside a poster showing the werewolf of the movie as a monster-in-progress, as he was making the transformation from man to beast. The man, the real man, lit a cigarette and threw the matchbook into the street. "He's not all that scary, Mary. He looks like somebody's father." Personally, I thought the poster was scarier.

"Maybe he is somebody's father. But I assure you he's also nuts."

When we handed the usher our tickets, the man in the hat approached the cashier. "Sit in the back row," Mary Parker whispered. And she sat beside me, on the aisle.

The man in the hat came in and sat in the row ahead of us, even though there were only three other people in the theater and there were plenty of empty seats to choose from. Once the lights went down, he sat kind of sideways, so he was half looking at us, half looking at the werewolf. "What's he doing?" I whispered.

Mary Parker turned to assess me in the dark. But all she said was, "Never mind."

The man in the hat stayed for only the first half of the double feature. Before *Shadow of the Cat*, he stood up and went by, leaning and whispering to Mary Parker as he passed. Up close, he didn't look so nice after all. "What did he say?" I whispered, turning to watch him amble toward the exit sign.

"He hissed."

"He hissed?"

She shrugged. "He hissed." And just then, the werewolf appeared again at the end of the credits and did the same thing on the screen. It lasted like an hour. It sent shivers down your spine.

We still watched *Shadow of the Cat,* though. Then we watched the entire double feature one more time. Then the usher told us that as far as young girls were concerned, the theater was closed.

It was dark outside. There were only a few people on the streets of downtown Cleveland, and they were either sitting or lying on them. "I wish I were old and rich," I said. "Then I'd give these people houses."

Mary Parker kind of laughed. "When you're old and rich, you won't, though."

I still thought I would. I just didn't say so.

As we walked, I kept looking over my shoulder, checking dark doorways, hoping not to find the werewolf from the movie clinging to the bars of a window, sprouting hair and fangs, howling in his transformational agony at the full moon. Then I looked straight ahead, and, crossing ahead of us, his long shadow cast in the light of a streetlamp—was the man in the hat. "Look," I said, stopping Mary Parker by the arm.

"Whoa. It's the wolf."

We ran twelve blocks to Terminal Tower, where we were the only people tearing down the platform to the train. Mary Parker got off at her stop, and I went on alone. But I thought how fear was the opposite of love the whole way home.

One of the garage doors was open, which was good because that meant Mother and Dad were already out. Saturday nights they often went to a cocktail party or an open house. When I once asked Mother what an "open house" was, she said it meant dinner would not be served. When I asked her then what was served, she said cocktails. But then I forgot to ask her what was the difference between a cocktail party and an open house.

She dressed the same for either one. And she always came to show Cabot and me before she left the house. We loved her party dresses. When we were younger, they had been flowing and full-skirted, now they were chic and short. But almost always when she was ready for the cocktail party or the open house, we said how she looked like a picture in a magazine. Cabot especially always said it. I figured that's why Cabot could only draw pictures of pictures of real people. I'd have to ask Mary Parker about that.

"Where've you been?" Clarine asked when she caught me trying to be clever by circling around after checking the garage and coming in the front door. You almost never got caught coming in the front door, because Clarine hardly ever hung out around there.

"With my friend."

"Then where's your friend been?"

I tried to slip past her. She snatched me by the arm.

"We kept trying to come home, but we were followed."

"By what?"

"A man in a hat."

Clarine's eyes widened into southern sunflower position, which they would do on special occasions. Then I told her about the double feature, and about watching it twice, just to make sure a certain man in a hat was gone. But I didn't tell her we saw him later in the light of a streetlamp, and I sure didn't tell her it all happened downtown.

Matt smelled trouble and came out of the library. He was seventeen now, and I suppose tall, dark, and handsome, because all the girls liked him. It was a nuisance, because they so often wanted to brainstorm with me about it. From the way he was all cleaned up and everything, you had to guess he was on his way out to break a few more hearts.

Clarine said, "No more picture shows for you, miss," and "Wait until your ma hears about this," but I suspected these were idle threats. She closed down her eyes and marched in full displeasure toward the back.

"Hey, who's your sexy friend?" Matt asked me. "I saw you guys downtown."

"Then how come you didn't say hello?"

"Because you were running."

"Oh."

"Why were you running?"

"Because we'd just robbed a store."

Matt just stood there. He had dark eyebrows, and he knew how to use them. But now they remained intentionally flat and unimpressed. He said, "Yeah, right."

Well, so what if he didn't believe me. We had robbed a store. Just as he had, actually: stealing the stuff and then putting it back.

He didn't own the patent on it. "So you thought my friend was sexy?"

"She looks like a cute little revolutionary."

"A cute little revolutionary?" I looked up. Cabot's long blond hair hung in loose curtains over the banister, making me regret the bobby pin girl. "Matt, seriously. Time to tell us what planet you are from."

I hesitated, for sure, but I asked them anyway. "So am I sexy?"

Luke sped through the hall, a football cradled in his arm, as if walking, but fast, toward a goalpost, because he wasn't allowed to run for touchdowns in the house. He said, "Too close to call." And was gone as fast as he came.

"I think you are." It was six-year-old Lucy in pajamas, joining Cabot on the landing.

"Thanks, Luce."

"That's okay."

"What's this nasty talk? Don't you know a baby when you see one?" Clarine appeared, scooped up Lucy and carried her back toward her room.

We all looked at one another. A baby? Let go, already, Clarine.

"Who'd you go with?" Cabot asked. "What revolutionary?"

"Mary Parker."

"You went with Mary Parker?" She was impressed. You could tell. "How did that happen?"

I said pointedly, "Because she heard you call me Zuzu at school." Which Cabot was strictly not supposed to do, though now I was pretty glad she had. But no point in letting her know that.

"I did? Sorry."

But then it reminded me, and since I had them together, I thought I'd better tell them the bad news about It's a Wonderful Life. "Did you guys know that the man in the movie Dad nicknamed me after is named George?"

Cabot said, "And?"

"Well, that's Dad's name."

Matt said, "George?"

Cabot said, "Yeah, Matt. You didn't know that?"

Luke cruised back in with his football and stopped. "I did."

Cabot said, "Good. Good, everybody. We all know Dad's name."

I said, "We're in big trouble, because this other George, you won't believe what he does."

Cabot said, "Well, he is the *other* George."

I said, "But there are already two people named after this movie in the family. How do we know there aren't more?"

Luke said, "What movie?"

Cabot said, "What's their last name in the movie?"

"Bailey."

"Then I wouldn't worry about it."

"But how do we know the whole *family's* not named after it? And Dad's trying to, like, *copy* it?"

Luke said, "What movie?"

Cabot said, "Because *she* named the boys. Dad only named us. If we had been boys, we would have been named Mark and John, so she could have the four guys who wrote the Bible. She was totally praying we would be boys."

Matt said, "She wasn't the only one."

Luke said, "What about Lucy?"

Cabot said instantly, "Peter, Paul, or Jude."

As per usual, they had an enormous knack for missing the point. "I'm just warning you, Dad thinks he's living in some movie where a guy named George loses everybody's money and tries to kill himself."

"Chill," Matt said. "It has a happy ending."

Cabot sighed. "I wish he'd talk about it."

"I'm just warning you. . . ."

"See you," Matt said, and started jingling the keys to a Buick.

Luke said, "What *movie?*" But I guess nobody wanted to talk about it anymore.

Monday morning at Assembly, she didn't even look at me. I figured she didn't want to make too big a deal over the fact that we'd done something together over the weekend. So I played it rather cool myself. Except in afternoon Assembly, when I broke down and wrote her a note: *My brother Matt saw us robbing Woolworth's and he thinks you're sexy.*

This is what Mary Parker wrote back: *Would you rather be, 1. As smart as Einstein, 2. As good as Gandhi, or 3. As beautiful as Scarlett O'Hara?*

I thought about it. After Saint Theresa and Mickey Knight, I'd already given up on beautiful. And after Mary Parker, I wasn't going for smart. So I finally circled "Good as Gandhi" and passed the note back up.

She passed it back. *Try again.*

That wasn't the right answer? I was surprised. But I wouldn't mind "Smart as Einstein," if she insisted, so I circled that and passed it back.

She wrote, *And again.*

I had no choice but to circle Scarlett O'Hara. I wrote beside it: *She's some old movie star, right?*

She wrote: *Meet me on the Rapid Transit at nine tomorrow morning.*

Tomorrow was a school day.

She turned around. "You'll be with me. I'll fake you a note."

So the next morning I lurked around, then left the house late and met Mary Parker on the Rapid Transit. She was wearing the same black outfit she had worn on Saturday, and her hair was back up in its ponytail. She had the movie we were going to see circled in red in the *Plain Dealer*. It was *Gone With the Wind*. "We had to see it today," she said. "It's a revival, and it's leaving Wednesday."

Silently, I began to account for the many days Mary Parker wasn't in school.

We watched the movie twice, but I still left the theater near tears. "She loses Rhett Butler, after all that," I sniffed, dabbing my eyes. "That's a terrible way to end a story."

"Nah, he'll come back to her in the sequel."

"He will?" He didn't seem like he would, with the way it ended, with the "Frankly, Scarlett, I don't give a damn." But as far as I knew so far, Mary Parker had never been wrong.

We were waiting for the Rapid Transit at Terminal Tower when Mary Parker suddenly asked me that same strange question again. Would I like to be as smart as Einstein, as good as Gandhi, or as beautiful as Scarlett O'Hara?

"As beautiful as Scarlett O'Hara."

Mary Parker smiled. "Even if she loses Rhett Butler in the end?"

"He's coming back to her in the sequel."

"Well, I can't guarantee that."

"You can't?"

Mary watched the Rapid approach through the dark tunnel and said, "There's only one guarantee. All stories end in death or marriage."

But I wasn't really listening because I was thinking ahead to the sequel. "All stories end in death or marriage," I repeated mindlessly.

"Some end in death *and* marriage."

"But there's still a sequel, right?" She didn't answer because the Rapid arrived.

•   •   •

On the train, I was staring out the window watching a cement wall fly by, thinking that Melanie died, and that was sad, though not as sad as what Rhett said to Scarlett, but it did make it a story that more or less ended in death or marriage, when Mary Parker turned to me and said, "So? Should I make you as beautiful as Scarlett O'Hara?"

I sort of smiled at Mary Parker.

"No joke. This is serious."

This was true. Nothing was more serious than the beauty of Scarlett O'Hara. I looked in Mary's cool brown eyes, wondering if what she had in mind was one of Mickey Knight's emotionally damaging Before and Afters. I didn't feel like telling her that despite the best beauty products money could buy, I just wasn't makeover material.

"Look, I'm not talking about a miracle here. You simply have to grow to understand your beauty comes from the inside out."

Oh. She was talking about that kind of beauty. She was talking modest, loving, and pure. The kind of beauty you find in the eyes. I had been quite clear from day one, I wanted the kind you found on your face.

"And what's inside?" Mary Parker continued. "Inside, you've got a heart and a mind. And, importantly"—here she pointed to a place somewhere below my neck, under my collarbone, to the right of my left arm—"a will. *That's* how you become beautiful. You *will* it. You can will yourself into anything. You can will yourself into the United States presidency if that's what you want. A lot of undeserving crackpots have."

I thought of my brother Matt.

Then Mary Parker told me she had been experimenting with will. She said she had developed a theory that a person could be, have, or accomplish anything she wanted if the person could just convince herself that she could be, have, or accomplish anything she wanted. She said the hard part was not doing the thing, but convincing yourself you could. She said the hard part was will.

"Sure. But what do you do about *that?*"

"Good. I'm glad you understand so far."

Then Mary Parker said she had invented a system of what she called "Parallel Actions," just "Parallels," for short. She explained that a Parallel was a tricky thing, but for the sake of argument, a thing not unlike a metaphor, in this case an action, through which you got the sense of accomplishing your objective by accomplishing a like objective, a similar objective, or a totally unlike objective to which you could still liken the feeling and emotional equivalent of your objective. She said these Parallels trained your will, taught it to get used to getting what it wanted, so it knew it could.

"I see," I said, because I sort of did. I told her about my own theory, how I wanted to stop poverty by making the thought of it unthinkable. "Could you do something like that?"

"Yes, yes," she said, getting pretty excited, for her. "Yes and no. It's the same principle. But I don't have much confidence in getting you to the point where you could stop poverty. For that I'd have to make you as good as Gandhi, as smart as Einstein, and probably as rich as Rockefeller. I'm not attempting the impossible here. You'll have to settle for being as beautiful as Scarlett O'Hara."

"Gee, I don't know . . ."

"Don't take me too literally, Boyce. What I am offering you, what I'm fairly sure I can give you, is a parallel persona to Scarlett O'Hara's. The total package. Brains, beauty, and a way with men."

I wanted to think about it, I guess.

While I did that, we rode along on the Rapid Transit and I stared at a strange hole in its floor. It wasn't a complete hole, you couldn't see the ground screeching by or anything, but you sure could hear it, and it did give you the feeling if you stepped a little too hard on that thin path, you might fall through a deep, dangerous hole. I thought, even if Mary Parker could do as she claims, it should be rather obvious why I cannot be part of the experiment. The key ingredient of Scarlett O'Hara's infamous "persona" *was* her beauty. And beauty was kind of out of the question for me. People didn't seem able to decide if I were pretty, or pretty unappealing. The consensus was, I looked like a choirboy.

"Well, okay, then," Mary Parker said, a little impatient. "You just let me know."

We rode along for quite a while. I didn't realize until later that Mary Parker had missed her stop, and now would have to get out and cross the tracks and take a Rapid Transit going back toward downtown. I guess I should have realized it, but I was quite absorbed with the thin patch on the Rapid floor, and the screeching sound of the metal wheels on the rusty old Transit tracks.

Finally I said, "Are we talking about good-looking, or what?"

"Yes, I mean physically beautiful."

"Okay, do you think that's even possible, under the circumstances?"

"See? That's the problem."

"Okay, even if I believe you, how are you going to make it happen?"

She brightened up. "The Parallel I've chosen for you is starvation."

"I'm not even fat!"

"It's the fat on your *brain* I'm worried about. It's keeping you from being what you could be."

This sounded like an insult, even though I knew it was science.

"For ten days, if you do it, you'll have only coffee, milk, and pipe tobacco. And you'll consume only books."

"Am I going to eat them?"

"Don't take me too literally, Boyce. Or Zu." She hesitated. "Do you mind if I call you Zuzu?"

I never could stand the wretched name, none of my friends used it, most of them didn't even know it, I'd made sure of that, but I kind of didn't hate the idea of Mary Parker using it because she actually knew what it meant, even if it only meant I was a three-year-old moron. So I finally said it was fine.

"So, Zuzu," she said, nodding and trying the new name out. "Listen up."

Then Mary Parker told me that in her experiments, she'd discovered that starvation of the body has a profound effect upon the will. She believed that the body welded with the will during starvation, that, in effect, the body fed off the will to sustain itself. Therefore, one's wishes or dreams, which Mary Parker considered of the will, would be "physicalized" through starvation. So, if I wished and dreamed and believed in being beautiful while simultaneously starving myself and reading good books, I would be beautiful! And soon too.

I said, "Why milk?"

"That's how babies do it. You're starting from scratch, see."

"Can't we just go with Gandhi? I think there's more potential in starvation there."

"Maybe we'll get to him later. I feel more comfortable starting you out on Scarlett O'Hara. This is all new ground, you understand."

"Sure, sure. Just as long as you don't mix them up. I'd hate to end up being as beautiful as Gandhi and as good as Scarlett O'Hara."

"Oh, don't worry about that. I'm going to oversee the experiment carefully. I've already selected your books."

"You have?" I really stared at that hole in the Rapid floor now.

"Your mind and your heart are, in essence, your will. I've checked you out, I wouldn't try this with anyone. I think your heart is in the right place."

That was a compliment, so I said, "Thanks."

"But your mind could stand, well, some enhancement."

Old Zuzu again. I was going to have to take this up with my father, for sure.

"Please listen carefully because I'm only going to say this once. Are you listening?"

I was a little startled at Mary Parker's deep seriousness. I nodded yes I was, and got ready to concentrate.

"I've chosen mostly philosophy and poetry for you to study, in some cases, memorize. I'm hoping you'll be able to search beyond the boundaries of the rational or known. I want you to reach past reason, because pure reason is confining and limits your imagination, thus your ability to create. And your major responsibility in life is the creation of your self. You can't do this successfully if you're limited to the rational. The books I've chosen will help you incorporate all that life is that you don't see, the part of life past consciousness. I can't tell you how crippling it is to accept only that which is made evident by observable fact and reason as the whole truth."

"So . . . to be beautiful, you believe I need books."

"Absolutely. You should also see lots of movies, though I'm not sure why. I think, maybe, because they perpetuate myth, and myth is an important part of your self-creation. And see them twice through, at the very least, at a sitting. And then go back and see them twice more. Of course, you don't have to do it. But it would be an important experiment for me."

I figured, whatever. Now that teenage life had thrown me into a kind of diminishing returns beauty contest with Mickey Knight and all my other drop-dead friends, I might as well give philosophy, poetry, cinema, and starvation a shot. "Okay. I'll do it."

"Good. One thing, though. I'm going to try to give you knowledge. But wisdom you'll have to get on your own."

I nodded. That was profound.

"And one other thing?"

I looked at her, waiting to hear something else to remember for life.

"If you want the persona we're talking about?"

"Yes?"

"You have to lose the crew cut."

My hand rose immediately to what there was of my hair.

So, because I believed then, as maybe I still do now, that there was no one smarter than Mary Parker, I allowed her to conduct her wild experiment on me. I began to starve myself, under her guidance. Each morning, I skipped breakfast at home, saying I had to go work on a special project at school. Then I skipped lunch at school. Then every day at four, I came shakily through the back door and listened for Clarine. She should be in the basement, doing laundry. Everybody else should be out doing sports. The boys should be practicing football or basketball. Cabot should be riding or taking tennis lessons. Lucy should be skating. Mother should be coaching any number of them, because Mother was the all-round best athlete in the family.

I'd take off my shoes and carry them into the kitchen, careful not to alert Clarine. Then I made my daily pot of coffee. At first I didn't know how to make coffee. At first I put eight tablespoons of coffee grounds into the basket, and one cup of water into the pot. Next Assembly, I passed a note up to Mary Parker, asking if I could switch to tea. But then she wrote down how to make coffee the real way, with eight tablespoons of coffee and *eight* cups of water.

If I wanted to, she turned around and whispered, I could throw in one for the pot. "One what?" I asked, plenty worried.

"Never mind." She grinned. "Either way, it'll make your hair grow."

So after I learned how to make coffee properly, I decided I even enjoyed it. I'd pour it into one of those mugs with the TV station call letters Dad was always bringing home because he was in advertising, sit at the breakfast room table and stare out the leaded windows into infinite space. I'd seen Mother and Clarine, both beautiful, do the exact same thing for years.

After my eight cups of coffee, it was time for my hand-rolled, pipe-tobacco cigar. I tiptoed from the kitchen to the library and and locked the door. Then I took an envelope from Mother's secretary and the tobacco pouch from Dad's desk. I cut off the flap of the envelope, then shaped that into a square. I folded the bottom of the square and sprinkled pipe tobacco into the crease. Then I rolled it and licked the gum on the envelope, ending up with a sort of huge, ecru cigar, sometimes with the words "Cranes" or "Tiffany & Company" engraved on the side. I slid this into the breast pocket of my uniform, slipped up the back stairs to my bathroom, opened the window, and lit up.

The beauty of it was, I was able to think so brilliantly. Four days into the experiment, I'd already found some very feasible answers to some of the very complex philosophical questions Mary Parker had posed to me. And I had my reading list to stimulate me further. Sartre. Nietzsche. Aristotle, Socrates, Kant, and others. Plus the poets. I read their great works in the bathroom, while smoking the ecru cigar.

After six days of experiment, I wasn't what you could call hungry, but I was what you could call high. I went through the paces at school, though often laughed inappropriately, cried inexplicably, and fell asleep at my desk uncontrollably. Then, as I lay awake at night, I felt my body feeding off itself, as Mary Parker had predicted it would, feeding from my heart, my mind. My will.

To avoid dinner at home, I claimed I had to go back to school to work on the special project. What I in fact did evenings was sneak around on the Rapid Transit to see movies two times with Mary Parker. We saw mostly old ones, at the revival house, but we saw new ones too, at the mall. We saw Katharine Hepburn, Cary Grant, Spencer Tracy, Bette Davis, Robert Redford, Dustin Hoffman, Al Pacino, and many more.

Clarine was the first to come right out and say I was stoned to my face. On the second to last day of the experiment—the "penultimate" one, I had learned from reading the fat dictionary on the list—she found me sitting in the breakfast room with eight mugs lined up in front of me, and a pot of coffee in my hand. I had noticed that no matter how carefully I measured the water and the coffee into the pot, it never seemed to come out to eight cups. So I had decided to conduct an experiment of my own. I had poured four test cups, and didn't have much coffee left in the pot, when Clarine suddenly appeared at the breakfast room door.

"That's *coffee* you're playing with," she said in a low, shocked whisper.

I smiled up at her. And tilted my head to the side like a cocker spaniel. After nine days on my Parallel, I felt like a cocker spaniel. A thin, brilliant cocker spaniel, but still a cocker spaniel. I must have worn a spaniel's expression of happy expectancy, and I still believe if Clarine hadn't entered the room at the very moment she did, I would have made an enduring discovery not only about the nature of coffee but also about the nature of reality as perceived by a small dog.

"That's *coffee*," she said for a shocked second time. But I just whimpered and cocked my head to the other side.

She snapped her fingers in front of my face.

I put the coffeepot down and smiled up at lovely Clarine. She was tall and immaculate, as usual, and, in her white uniform, maybe not unlike a spaniel's vision of God. My eyes widened attentively, my ears lay back on my head.

She leaned over the table and peered into the cups. "You're not *drinking* it, are you?"

I pawed at a mug, managed to pick it up and offer it to her.

She scoffed at it, even though she had a bit of a coffee habit herself. "Explain yourself, young lady. You know you're not permitted to drink that trash."

Trash. I shrugged into the cup.

Then something strange happened. While Clarine rattled off about a billion reasons why I wasn't supposed to drink coffee aka trash, including growth stunting, growth spurting, heart stopping, heart racing, suddenly her voice started sounding real slow and way way underwater. "Clarine," I interrupted, "you sound really *southern*."

"What? Whas' the matter with you, girl?"

"*See!?*" I cried.

Then, what I did, I started sounding really southern myself. It was like when they say your life flashes before your eyes before you die, but they say it flashes really slowly, so slowly you have all kinds of time to look it over, and it gets so dull and boring it's like a three-hour movie but just not a good one, and you totally want to die. And they say that takes the edge off the actual dying. That's how slow I suddenly sounded.

Clarine gaped at me in astonishment. "Are you *mocking* me, girl?"

"I'm on a Parallel!" I blurted in my own defense.

"You're on a parallel," Clarine repeated, nodding her head. "I see. Then I do see. You're on a parallel *what?*"

"Jus' a Parall'l," I mumbled, very southern, growing very worried that I'd let the secret slip. In the tradition of all great experiments, no one was supposed to know.

"Well, lemme see now. You on 'parall'l' *bars?* You on 'parall'l' *planes?* Or are you just on a 'parall'l' *universe?* Huh? Just what type of 'parall'l' do you think you mean?"

Now who was mocking who. Whom. I scowled up at her. "Just let me *think.*"

While I did, I searched Clarine's beautiful brown eyes, not unlike pools of coffee themselves. Then, as if from a great, slow distance, the thought I had been waiting for suddenly arrived like a locomotive in my head. I had been waiting for it for over a week. It was the answer to a major philosophical question about the nature of reality, and when I had the thought clearly in hand, I grinned at Clarine and decided to give it to her as a peace offering. I started to speak, but no sound came out of my mouth. I looked miserably into a coffee mug and looked back up. A terrifying frown had now inhabited Clarine's face.

I started to speak again, but no sound came out again. I tried once more, but all that came out was a growl. I didn't sound southern anymore. I sounded like a cocker spaniel.

"What's the matter with you, child?" Clarine studied me with a look of amazement on her face, as if she had just noticed that I sometimes elongate or contract. Meanwhile, I kept forming very distinct yet soundless words with my mouth.

"Speak up," she said, nodding her head, then shaking it sideways, as if encouraging an infant or an animal to try to articulate. "You sure look strange, and different," she finally said.

"CLARINE!" I said, way too loudly. There.

"Clarine," I said, modulating. "Did you know that all knowledge of reality . . . that if you take the empirical world . . . that is that pure logical thinking . . . that, that, that you can't *get* it that way?"

Rats. I blinked up at Clarine, feeling robbed.

Clarine drew herself up, waited, and delivered. "WELL, HOW DO YOU DO, MISTER EINSTEIN."

Oh no.

"*That* who you think you are, Miss Smarty Pants?"

I adamantly shook my head. The last thing you wanted was Clarine saying she thought you thought you were Einstein.

"*Pure logical thinking cannot yield us any knowledge of the empirical world.* Is that what you're trying to spit out, Miss Intelligence? I'm afraid that one belongs to Mister Einstein."

Very surprisingly, "Pure logical thinking cannot yield us any knowledge of the empirical world" was totally what I had been trying to say. I was quite taken aback that Clarine, not to mention Einstein, had said it first.

"I know that one. You've been acting so strange, I took a good look at those books you've got your nose buried in. You had the one about pure logical thinking highlighted in every color in the rainbow. It made it look like *mud*."

"That *isn't* what I was trying to say at all," I lied imperiously.

Clarine leaned into my face, spent a good ten seconds searching my eyes, and concluded her investigation by pounding the breakfast room table with her fist. "Well, I've been doing some logical thinking for myself," she said. "And you know what my logical thinking is saying to me?"

I shook my head no, but I was pretty scared to hear it.

"That you've been smoking reefer! *That's* what."

• • •

Then she examined me. My eyes, my ears, my uniform. She grabbed my school blazer off the chair and went through the pockets. Luckily I hadn't yet rolled my ecru cigar. She dropped the blazer and frisked my jumper. Then she went for my knee socks.

Finally, she made a slow circle around the table, then suddenly came up from behind and lunged for my wrist. She picked up my arm. "Look here, how thin." She dropped my arm. It flopped on the table.

She came around front again and started staring at it as if she couldn't stop. So I got interested in it myself and started staring at it too. There we were in the breakfast room, staring at my arm.

Finally, she picked it up again, and carefully turned it over, and over again. She looked into my eyes. I looked into hers. We both looked back at the arm. I think it was at that moment that we both realized: what we were dealing with here was the surprisingly graceful arm of a young woman, no longer to be confused with a choirboy, or even a choirgirl.

I felt an intense thrill of total recognition. The experiment had *worked*.

As she put my arm respectfully back on the table, "Why baby, you're all grown up" was all Clarine said.

Not that that was the last of it. There followed an intense period of surveillance wherein I had to eat almost constantly while Clarine milled around with arms crossed and watched me stuff face, plus I had to convince both her and Matt behind closed breakfast room doors that I was not some kind of junkie. I think Matt had been called in for his supposed authority on the subject of "reefer," which sure made the burden of proof a lot easier on me.

Guarding my best friend's secret, I explained away my unusual behavior and dramatic change in appearance as perfectly natural, considering my coming of age. That I billed as strictly time lapse, total rapid transit. What with my abstruse references to the tenuous nature of reality and the importance of redefining the empirical world, eventually, they both bought it. Although, to be honest, Clarine did outdebate me, and definitely Matt, on several key philosophical points.

In between bouts in the breakfast room, I headed to my bathroom to gaze at myself in the mirror. What I saw there, I really wanted to be real.

I was beautiful. No, not beautiful.

"[Boyce Parkman] was not beautiful, but men seldom realized it when caught by her charms . . . ." Almost verbatim the way Scarlett O'Hara's story was written.

It was only then that I began to fully appreciate the genius of Mary Parker.

Not only had she made me beautiful, she had made me brave. Fear, she had taught me, was the opposite of love. The heart and mind is will. All stories end in death or marriage. All happy families are alike. . . . And pure logical thinking cannot yield us any knowledge of the empirical world.

SIXTEEN

It's summer after such a sorry sequence of events I suppose I shouldn't even think about it, but I suppose I shouldn't have ended up looking like Lolita either. I've been sent to Florida for it, in the summer, and if that sounds pleasant, it's really just a polite way for Mother to say, Go roast in hell.

After Mary Parker's experiment ended, my lips kept on going. They grew fuller and fuller until I finally had to go to Mary Parker and ask, "Is this like a quirk?"

But Mary Parker said not to worry, that very full lips could be a very good sign, that they could signify the lush, outward expression of a flowering, inner expressive self. I thought that made my lips sound nice.

But Mother didn't think they were nice. First she accused me of pouting. Then she said I was trying my best to look like a "tart." I had to ask her what a tart was, as I'd always thought it was either a rather attractive French pie, or a small turnover Clarine let you make from leftover pastry dough when you were little. Mother wouldn't answer me though. I had to ask Mary Parker. I wasn't too flattered when I heard the additional definition either.

I joked to Cabot that my lips seemed to be causing a "flap." Of course I knew it wasn't funny when I said it, but that's the very reason Cabot was supposed to laugh. That's the way we do it, the way it had always been done. But Cabot just said she'd give me an even fatter lip if I didn't stop looking at them in the mirror. Matt, for once on my side, said I looked hot, except he said it a lot, a lot in front of Mother, and of course that wasn't too constructive. But that's just Matt.

Everyone had an opinion about my lips, because nothing can happen at home without everyone having an opinion about it. Except Dad. Actually, he sort of had one too. After I got caught for using my new lips to kiss Rey McDowell, he had a talk with me in the library. But all he said was "Boyce, it's come to my attention that you're a very pretty girl." Then he said it's best not to drink on dates. In the future of course. When it was legal.

Where I am is on a balcony on a kind of McMansion in Florida, where mostly what I do is sit in a deck chair at night and stare like a zombie at the full moon. It's out there now surfing on a wave, hanging ten, falling all over itself doing the old razzle-dazzle soft-shoe hard sell that it's supposed to be paradise here. Someone should put it out of its misery.

The McMansion is Mickey Knight's, and of course her father's, the brain surgeon. Mother got the idea to send me down here for the summer after she found out Mickey Knight was no longer my best friend; Mary Parker, the bus driver's daughter was. She also found out about skipping class and going to the million movies downtown. For that I will be sent to boarding school in the fall.

Meanwhile I'm banished here to the McMansion with Mickey Knight and her father, who's nicknamed "The General," though nobody tells why. "The Admiral" would be more like it, since he spends all his time on a boat, killing fish. I have to go with him and Mickey tomorrow morning at five AM to kill some myself, and I'm so worried about all the carnage, I can't sleep.

• • •

So since I'm up anyway, I've been thinking of doing some thinking. Not logical thinking, of course. I'll think everything through illogically. Then I'll be all set for later in life and the real world, when I'm not banished to a McMansion anymore.

At the top of the list is Dad, like what's his story, and at the bottom, after Matt, is my lips. Frankly, I kind of liked the way Cabot said she'd give me an even fatter lip. I actually liked that. Of course I didn't tell her so, but I think of it sometimes. I miss Cabot and Clarine especially, and little Lucy maybe even a little more, and even Matt quite a lot come to think of it, and of course Luke. He's such a nice kid, and so eager and stuff, with his baseball mitt and his football and his big plans to go play the game, you couldn't help but miss Luke. I'm not sure I miss Mother, though. And Dad, I'm putting him in limbo, since he could have come to my rescue but instead had a Scotch.

Cabot said I was really missing what was actually happening with our family because I was blinded from looking in mirrors. It's kind of embarrassing to be told that. Even though I secretly liked the fat lip thing, I was sort of embarrassed about that other part of it. I mean, I was just looking. But maybe that's bad, and that's why I worked up this list for thinking tonight.

Dad did this strange thing in spring. He sold a blue Buick. I found out when Cabot came to my room and said in a tragic voice, "Dad lost a Buick."

That killed me, when she said that. How do you lose a Buick? I knew what she was talking about, but I still made her tell me how you lose a Buick, like please spell that out for me, I'm deeply confused. Maybe it's still at the mall? Did you check the airport? She said it meant he had to sell it because he needed money.

So that's how you lose a Buick, I said. I have to admit, I was fairly sarcastic about it.

But Cabot still went around moaning that Dad lost a Buick. I told her she had too much imagination and all, that she better use it instead to sketch pictures of pictures of real people—that is, beautiful models from magazines—at which I already said she is very good.

Except the next time I found her sketching, she was doing ugly people, disjointed people, tormented people, with things like triangles for heads. She explained it by claiming she was "into reality," though personally I thought the beautiful models more real. Anyway, the way she kept moaning how Dad "lost" a Buick, even if you didn't believe her, it might still make you plan to think about that.

Then something else happened concerning one of the cars. Dad accidentally sort of burned up the Dream Machine. It happened when he finally drove it to work in downtown Cleveland. Before that, he'd tried it out on little hops up the road, but on any errand of consequence, he'd still always defer to one of the two remaining blue Buicks.

But one Friday, he must have decided to form some sort of permanent bond with his father's old white Mercury, because he took off in it for work in downtown Cleveland. And he looked confident too, going down the driveway.

As he always did with a blue Buick, he parked in the Terminal Tower's underground garage. But he must have been a little ambivalent about the whole bonding thing, because just as he was about to climb out of the Dream Machine, Dad fumbled his cigarette. Then he neglected to pick up the part that was lit.

When Dad returned to the garage at five-thirty that afternoon, he was greeted by an exhilarated garage attendant with a smudged face and a charred jumpsuit who described in detail his heroic rescue of the smoldering car. They towed it home and put it back in its slot in the four-car garage. We all tromped out to see it. It looked like an ash.

After dinner that night, Matt told a little circle of us that Dad had tried to "torch" the Dream Machine. Wide-eyed, we asked what he meant. "I mean *arson*," he said, blowing it out long, as if exhaling fire. "Your Dad's going nuts."

Now he was *our* Dad. Classic Matt.

"Rrrrr-son," Matt said again, extra long.

Cabot said, "Who are you? Satan?"

Luke said, "You're scaring me, Matt."

Lucy, highly offended, said, "Maybe *you're* nuts."

Me, I stayed out of it. I thought he might have a point.

Then Dad sold his concert grand Steinway piano. But Matt didn't claim he was crazy and Cabot didn't claim he did it for money. We all knew the real reason why. His friend Mr. Carter had died. I would have sold the Steinway too. Anybody would have.

Mr. Carter had been coming Saturdays in his old Ford to visit Dad since we were babies. He came to play the saxophone while Dad played the piano. I had fallen in love with him when I was two, the minute I first saw him. Every time he came to the house carrying his sax, I would run and jump on top of him. If he sat down, I would crawl onto his lap. If he stood up, I would cling to his leg. If he tried to go, I would drag behind him, attached to his hand, his coattail, whatever I lucked onto that day. When he played his sax, I sat next to my father on the piano bench, gazing up at his fabulous friend, my feet kicking in time over the edge of the bench, my hands alternately reaching for his shiny brass instrument and plunging deep into the folds of my dress.

"She's developing an ear for music," Dad told Mother proudly, his fingers dancing all the way down the keyboard.

But Mother knew better. She repeatedly made the trip to the end of the living room to lift me off the piano bench, or pry me off Mr. Carter. Finally she squeezed my arms and looked in my eyes and ordered me to no longer glue myself to our guest. From then on, I spent Saturdays piled in a heap at his feet. And now, fourteen years later, he had died.

So we knew it was in honor of Mr. Carter that Dad sold the Steinway. But it wasn't just Saturdays that were quieter now. Dad was. He went to the library every night after work and had Scotch. But then he'd come out for dinner in a pretty good mood.

The moon has now hopped off that wave and is sitting on top of a palm tree down the beach like a smug white coconut.

Reclining here every night on my deck chair on my bedroom balcony like this, I'm kind of hoping I look like I've rather had a breakdown. I have a summer lap blanket tucked over my legs and the white curtain from my room billows out from the door, fluttering loose like an unhinged sail. My hair, now way past my shoulders, flies in the wind. I'm hoping if anyone passes by on the beach and sees me, they'll think I've been sent here to recuperate, to breathe the salt air from a deck chair and stare at the open sea as if I've just come out of a coma. I'm hoping they think, Too tragic, too young.

I got caught for kissing Reynolds McDowell after the spring dance at the Shaker Heights Country Club. Rey is Matt's friend who lives up the street. I've known him since he came to my crib and gave me a ball peen hammer to play with. Now he's tall and cool and has blue eyes that widen when he talks, but especially when you talk. I think his expanding eyes kind of give him away, like he's not so cool as you think, which personally I think is extra cool. I know I love him now, but I still say it was Mother's fault I had to keep kissing him to find out for sure. Mother had always said when the man you thought you loved first kissed you, you'd feel this very definitive electric shock. Sort of a zap. And that's how you'd know.

The dance was outside because of spring and there were heated tents and live music and old chaperones who sat in the dead white men's portrait room in the clubhouse drinking themselves under the table. Outside was for junior members and their friends and one friend of Rey's was a southern boy named Calhoun who wore a seersucker jacket with battered jeans and made mint juleps in the parking lot off the back of his rusty blue pickup truck. So Rey brought a couple of Calhoun's special drinks. Then we slipped away from the pickup, and took off our shoes for the grass.

When Rey kissed me on the golf course everything was slightly out of focus and distant and pretty, the lights strung along the inside of the white canvas tents and the music and the feel of his mouth on my cheek.

That was the problem, only on the cheek. Rey has a reputation for being what's sometimes called a lady-killer, but that's all he tried to lady-kill me. So I kept touching my face, trying to decide if I'd felt the supposed very definitive electric shock, and therefore was truly in love.

After we took our shoes and went back to the tent and the whole rest of the dance too, I kept trying to decide if I'd felt the very definitive electric shock, or what. I realized Rey would have to kiss me again or I would never be sure.

We were quite late coming home. Rey drove me, and then parked his father's Oldsmobile five hundred feet from the entrance to our driveway, behind the azalea bushes. But he still didn't lady-kill me. Instead he killed the lights, slowly and mysteriously put a finger to his lips, and opened his door. "What is it?" I whispered. "Why are we stopped way over here?"

"Why else. Your mother."

Oh. Then this was actually a very good idea. This way, Mother, who waited on the front stair landing every dance for me to come home, couldn't possibly hear the car. I could just slip in the back door and up the back stairs and go to sleep, and if when I woke in the morning I found Mother still on the landing, I could just say very sleepily and very innocently, "Gee, Mom, why are you hanging out there?"

It would have worked. It was my own fault that it didn't. Just as Rey was about to climb out of the car, I got extremely curious again about the very definitive electric shock. Rey apparently had no plans to kiss me again, so instead I leaned over and kissed him, just like he had done to me, on the cheek. Then I drew back, trying to decide if I had been zapped.

Rey had an odd reaction. After I kissed him, he sat with his head slumped, staring at the steering wheel. I thought I'd hurt him or something. I asked if he was okay and he shook his head no, then slumped it again. Finally he came to life and groped for the door handle, but then his hand sort of slid down. The hand went into the air and landed on the steering wheel, then it slid off. Then it came up and was on my face, and his mouth was on my mouth, and didn't slide off. And it was kind of eternal almost, except in the most exquisite middle of it, Rey leapt about ten feet out of the car. "Honey, I'm taking you home."

He'd called me Honey. I felt a very definitive electric shock.

At the back door, Rey forgot all about Mother and any more good ideas. I was halfway in the door, but he pulled me back out. Then I was up against the house, and his mouth tasted of sugar and bourbon and mint, from Calhoun's juleps. I somehow remembered what Rey forgot and I pulled myself away and ran in the door.

It still might have worked. But I had one bare foot safely on the back stairs, my slingback shoes slung over my finger, when I suddenly became very curious. Mother wasn't crazy enough to still be on the landing at this hour, was she? She would have given up and gone to bed, wouldn't she? She would have decided to deal with me in the morning, right?

I opened the front hall door a crack, slipped in to adjust to the darkness, and squinted up at the landing. And she wasn't there. I got a little bolder. I tiptoed to the bottom of the stairs, looked up at the landing, and she still wasn't there. And that satisfied my curiosity: my mother wasn't crazy. So what I did, I took the path of least resistance. Rather than go to all the trouble of turning around and going with the back stairs and the original plan, I slung my finger with the shoes over my shoulder and simply cruised right up the front stairs. And there on the landing from the shadows near the curtains, here came my mother, pouncing on me like a panther.

I'm not going into it further. It's too scary. But I got severely shaken by the shoulders, rocked, sort of back and forth like a rocking horse getting a good workout from a kid who didn't like it anymore. It wasn't painful or anything, but each time I rocked forth, it was closer to Mother's face, and she started sniffing. I tried to rock back when I realized, but it was too late. She had already sniffed out the kisses laced with bourbon and mint. Then there was that chat with Dad in the library, and, later that very week, the badly timed call from the headmistress at school. And almost the next thing I knew, I was here at the McMansion.

I'm getting quite carried away with this breakdown idea. Maybe if I can manage one, I won't have to go to boarding school in the fall. But the truth is, I'm wondering if I already had a sort of breakdown of sorts. I guess I know when it happened. It was after Mr. Carter died. I awoke in the middle of the night and remembered. And it didn't feel right to just go back to sleep. I had once loved him, after all. Even though I was two and he was over fifty, I had. And now he had died, and it seemed something should be done, some special honor should be paid, but I didn't know what. So I got out of bed and went downstairs in the dark.

I roamed around for a while, through the dining room and the living room. I sat down at the piano, since Dad hadn't sold it yet. I pretended to play the keys. But the imaginary music I made from memories of him there didn't seem to hold any answers, so I started roaming around again. I guess I couldn't find what I was looking for in the house, so then I pulled a sweater from a peg in the back hall and I drifted outside.

I flicked on the outdoor lights and walked down to the reflection pool with the naked Little-Boy Statue, and looked back up at the house. All the windows were dark and the house looked exceptionally spooky and large. Then, for no real reason, I headed for the garage and when I got there I rolled up all four of its doors.

There were two Buicks left, plus the Dream Machine, now completely restored and repainted, from the time Dad had torched it.

I finished opening garage doors and started walking back and forth in front of all the cars, as if I were a teacher or something, a teacher on the verge of giving a meaningful lecture on the final day of school. But I wasn't talking at the moment, because I was thinking up what I was planning to say. Then I paused, just like some teachers, for dramatic effect. But I started walking again when I couldn't think what was meaningful to say. I could almost hear the cars, like kids, collectively sigh. I figured it must be pretty tough to be a car parked in a garage, and then to get hit with a bad teacher on top of it all.

I continued pacing back and forth in front of all the cars. I was remembering a poem Mary Parker had assigned back during the experiment. It was about a flower in a "crannied wall" and the poet, he goes and plucks the flower, and holds it and looks at it there in his hand. Then the poet says, "Flower, but if I could understand what you are, root and all, and all in all, I should know what God and man is." Mary Parker had urged me to commit that poem to memory, as she said it held a simple but all-important principle, a principle that could be applied to anything in the world. She said that's what a true principle did, because it was universal.

So now I was thinking, What about things such as Dream Machines and blue Buicks? Could the universal principle be applied to a family car?

I began walking faster, thinking, it's a universal principle. If I could understand what you are, root and all and all in all, I would know what God and man is. I kept going back and forth, walking faster and faster in front of the cars in the garage.

Then I stopped short, with this fantastic idea to wave to all the cars or something, in the manner you might to a bunch of horses in a corral, as if you knew for a fact the barn was burning and were imploring the horses to get out of there while the going was good.

But then I didn't do that. I thought if I did, it would be proof I was having a breakdown.

I got so worried about going crazy and having a breakdown I began pretending instead it was just some sort of game, to find the meaning of things. I tried to pretend it was just a dumb game. Like a dumb game show, the type of game show where you win a car if you pick the right door, except I was making it so that the car that could reveal its meaning, root and all and all in all, would win.

Then I realized that this game show wouldn't even work, because the way I had set it up, the contestants were also the prizes. I thought I was going crazy.

Besides, deep down, I was fairly sure this wasn't any game I was playing. No matter how worried I got about going crazy, I just couldn't convince myself it was a game. So I decided that even if I went crazy, at least I wouldn't make finding the meaning to things just a dumb game.

So I started pacing again. There was the white Mercury, in the middle, and the Buicks, blank as anything, remote and unrevealing as only the blue Buick can be. They weren't pricey pink Cadillacs, after all. They weren't showy silver Jaguars. They weren't basic black Fords or flashy red Porsches or tinny green Chevrolets. They were solid, dull, incomprehensible, intractable, unyielding blue Buicks. A conspicuous display of nothing I knew of.

And then I just stopped and stared at the Mercury. And then I was almost sure I wasn't going crazy anymore. I stood there very still, worried if I moved a muscle, the meaning would go, because it seemed very fragile, this meaning, very delicate, like a flower. Then I figured at least I knew what the Mercury was supposed to mean. It meant memory. My grandfather. How things stood for things.

Grandfather had been clean and kindly looking, just like his car. He had been old, just like his car. I guess he had been just like his car. Mr. Carter had driven an old Ford, and he had been black and probably poor, but the two men didn't seem too different at all. Grandfather had had his snappy way of talking, calling his car a Dream Machine and you a Hot Ticket, and Mr. Carter had had his saxophone, so maybe it was something about the delightful sounds they made that made them seem similar. That would mean something, to a child.

That's when you knew it was good to have a grandfather's Dream Machine parked in the four-car garage. It was as if the car had survived death itself, and had come back to sit there, stubbornly symbolizing something.

I went and sat in the Dream Machine, flicked on the headlights and turned the ivory steering wheel, practicing. I decided that when I had my permit, this is the only car I would drive. I sat there for a long time, thinking of everything I was fairly sure I knew, up until now, trying to concentrate, in honor of Mr. Carter and all.

Then I fell asleep, and then Rey McDowell was there.

"I saw lights," he said, tapping on the windshield.

I opened up, and he climbed in.

He pressed the headlights off. "You'll run your battery down." Then he kissed me again, a lot this time, as if we were parked somewhere.

Kissed my lips. I think I'll go inside and take a look at them now.

WOMANHOOD

I have to admit it was almost fine for a while, being out at sunrise with the water so pure and smooth beneath the hull of the speeding boat.

I leaned out and reached my hand to touch the spray, trying to commit to memory certain things that can easily slip your mind about the water, like how it feels on your hand, and how vast it is, and how, with its billions of drops, it's still made out of parts and isn't one single thing, which is so easy to forget, at least I forget it all the time.

But then we rode way out beyond the sand bar, and when The General cut the engine and hurled the anchor overboard, the boat began to roll erratically, both side to side, and front to stern. This wasn't how we anchored with my father in a sailboat. Dad found a smooth cove or a harbor, and then he would drop anchor over the bow, slowly back up to secure it, and then we would just rock a little bit, which you didn't even notice after a while. But then I remembered: we were here to kill fish.

"He's making us bait our own hooks," Mickey said, basking in her deck chair in her black bathing suit. She got up and went over and stared into the bucket of squirming, pumping, muscling live bait. "Unbelievable."

I'd already done that, stared in the bait bucket. Now I was staring at The General. You couldn't see his eyes behind his Ray•Bans, but you could see his jaw was set all solid and his mouth all clamped down. He made a motion to get up from our chairs. There was clearly going to be a fish lesson now.

"Okay, girls. Line up and I'll show you how it's done."

Nobody did it. Line up, that is. I stood up, though. I mean I had to, he wasn't my father.

"Come on over here, Boy." That's what he called me, for short. Ever since I was six years old.

The General thrust his hand into the bait bucket and I watched in horror as he inserted a fishhook into the back of a shrimp. "Baiting builds character, girls."

I thought I had built enough character just to get on the boat at five AM, but all I said was "Yes, sir." He nodded too, and I took a tiny step closer.

He reached for my arm and slapped a wet shrimp in my palm. I closed my hand around it; it slimed out of my fingers and dropped to the deck. The General picked it up and slapped it back in my hand. "Now hook it decisively, Boy, right down the spine. Or they'll steal it from you. That's the first thing to know. Fish steal."

Lesson number one: fish steal.

I baited the hook.

I probably shouldn't have, it probably hurt the shrimp, it was probably going to kill the shrimp, not to mention the fish that would eat it and thus eat the hook, but I did as I was told. I suppose, I wouldn't have done it if it were a slightly larger animal. Like a lion or something. I suppose The General wouldn't have either. That's when I realized: the world was not fair. But all I did about it was do it. And then all I said was, "There."

The General inspected my hook. "Go deeper next time."

"Yes, sir." I liked calling him "sir," don't ask me why. It's what we had in common. I liked calling him "sir," and he liked calling me "Boy." And of course, we had Mickey Knight, his daughter and only child.

Now it was Mickey's turn. She stood up, grabbed the rod, and stabbed the shrimp's spine quickly, going way deep. Then she sat down again, holding the rod at an insolent angle, looking tan, beautiful, and royally bored.

"Hey," I said, watching the shrimp squirm in agony on the end of her line. "That was good."

"Unbelievable," she sighed.

"Come, Boy." The General took me astern and gave me a private lesson in casting, which Mickey, of course, had already had. The whole point of it was to hold onto the rod the whole time and not go with your instincts and throw it into the water along with the line. The General had me do it over and over, until he said, "Not bad."

And then we went fishing. And then, nothing happened. I didn't catch fish. Nobody did. I'd heard this very thing about fishing, that it takes annoying amounts of valuable time.

Finally I looked at The General to see what was wrong. But he was busy tending his six different rods, which he'd placed in gleaming stainless-steel brackets along what's called the gunwale, I think. But maybe that's what it's called on a sailboat. I was wondering it, I really was, but The General was so busy not catching fish, I didn't want to interrupt and ask.

It was some boat we were on, now that I had all kinds of time to look around. It was sleek and shiny and had techy things that whirred and clicked everywhere. There was a chair facing out at the water where you sat for big fish, if you were that far advanced. It had a seat belt, because without it, a big fish could pull you right overboard and catch you. Back home, The General had things like twin high-gloss Jaguars parked in his garage. Unlike my father, I guess he liked things that looked fresh out of the box. My father didn't like his things until they were broken in, and he liked them even better when they were all beaten up and way worn down.

It seemed hours before they actually got started, but when the fish finally started coming, The General was quite entertaining to watch. At least now you could guess why they called him The General. He went running from rod to rod as if dodging transparent bullets and winning invisible wars. Each newly captured fish was like a trophy or medal to him, which he held at eye level and admired. Then he tired of it quickly, threw it in a bin, and went back into action, capturing more.

My father had tried fishing once, off the sailboat, so we could have fish for lunch that day. He wasn't too good at it, though. We ended up having taco chips. Now, watching The General speed-sort his fish into individual bins, the yellowtails, the grouper, the snappers, I began to wonder if there was something lacking in my father for not catching fish. It seemed The General's ability to slay fish somehow embodied the very meaning of success. Even if I didn't adore the senseless murder involved, it did make my father's fishing seem pretty sad.

I looked over at Mickey and it was like father, like daughter. Already, she had her own bin of fish. She didn't seem too crazy about it, though. Every once in a while she'd say, "Okay, I've got one," but then she didn't act as if it were any Big Deal. She'd just reel each new fish in and unhook it, looking at it as if she already knew it, and wasn't too thrilled about seeing it back so soon. But she was doing it. At least she knew she could if she tried.

I started to not like the way I was beginning to feel about fish. Because I was beginning to want to kill them too. But they were too smart to let me. I was doing exactly what Mickey and her father were doing: baiting the hook with the live shrimp, then casting the line without throwing the rod. But the fish just took my bait and swam away. By the way, fish steal. I'm not saying they don't deserve to, but they're not above it, is all. Anyway, it was beginning to seem like some kind of family problem, not to be able to outsmart a fish. At home, unlike at The General's houses, we didn't have one fish on our walls.

The sun was now fire, cooking the chub in the pails, which now reeked. The boat had never stopped pitching side to side, front to stern.

I was using something else for bait now, something called chum, which at least was already chopped up, already dead. The General's fish had eaten all the live bait, except for a few prize shrimp, which he gallantly offered to me and which I politely declined.

But the fish didn't want my chum either. They snubbed my line altogether now, perhaps insulted by this chopped-up, dead chub, which The General said was "just a member of the Carp Family, Boy." When he said that, I felt sorry for the Carp Family, whoever they were.

"You don't have the heart for it," The General said.

Hey, I knew what "heart" meant, because of Matt. Heart was the thing great boxers had, what kept them going when they had nothing else left. Or soldiers. In the vocabulary of violence, or was it in fact the vocabulary of success, or merely the vocabulary of sport, but in any vocabulary at all, wasn't "heart" distinguished from "killer instinct"?

"It's your attitude," said Mickey, counting dead fish. "I've never seen anyone catch *no* fish. Not on *this* boat. Right, Dad?"

Complaining of third-degree burns, I fixed my baited rod into one of those fancy clamps on what I think's called the gunwale, leaving my line in the water, just in case.

There were three berths below. I chose the V-berth and lay down. I really felt woozy and weak. I wondered whether I should try to make it to the head, or just stick my head through the porthole and throw up.

But then, don't ask me why, maybe it was sunstroke or something, but I started crying instead. I began to think it was really sad how the one time he tried to catch a fish, off the sailboat, with the crude rod he just rigged up from things on the boat and the bread we had in the galley for bait, that that one time he tried, my father didn't catch one fish. That he'd just had the idea that he would catch a fish and thought that the idea would catch one. That struck me as so sad, so innocent now. Fathers could kill you with their sad innocence.

But I, innocently, had thought my father would catch a fish that day too. I sat there in the cockpit with him and hoped to God it would happen, and every time the line jerked my heart leapt up and I hoped it was a fish.

But when Dad laughed and gave up, I didn't cry. And I knew now that if he had really wanted to catch a fish he could have just gone and bought a good rod and some live shrimp and then he would have had what he needed to do it. He could have persisted. He could have learned. But maybe he was unconvinced about the very idea. Maybe he reasoned, what would it bring, in the end? So you get a great fish, a trophy to hang on your wall. Would it be worth it, for the dodgy thing you had to do?

Then, just at that moment, I wished more than anything I could go home, see my father, and maybe even bring him something, like a nice fish.

• • •

I dried my eyes on the end of my tee shirt. Then I started crying again, because once you find one thing to cry about, like fish, they start coming in schools. I started crying for all the fish that had died that day, the way they gawked at you while they were dying, so flabbergasted at your senselessness they couldn't even blink their eyes. But then I kept crying, probably beyond any sincere pity I could have possibly felt for fish. Maybe I was having that breakdown, but I knew I had to be quiet about it, because Mickey and her father were right up on deck.

Then my sorrow for fish turned to sorrow over war, poverty, and the fact that Mary Parker's father was a bus driver. That just seemed so sad, so innocent, somehow. To drive a bus. To simply and honorably just get people where they're supposed to go. I started thinking of that, and of all the bus drivers all over the world, in countries that were packed with buses and packed with people in the buses, and then I couldn't stop.

"Boyce!"

It was Mickey's voice. I stopped crying immediately, I mean I had to, you could never explain crying over all the bus drivers at this late date, and I pretended I was asleep.

"Come up here right now!" I rubbed my eyes and saw Mickey rocking above me in what I think's called the companionway.

"Guess what? There's a fish or something on your line."

Really? A fish or something?

"Step lively, Boy! Or he'll get away!"

"So are you *coming?*"

Up on deck, The General was already handling my rod. But he turned it over to me immediately, so I could reel in my own catch.

"Keep it up, up like this," The General said, "without any slack, or it will snatch the bait and swim away."

I did that, I did just as he said.

"Turn the reel, slowly, slow, steady . . ."

I did it. Then there was a tug, a pull, a brief fight at the end. And then the fish flew out of the water.

I saw my fish, and I already knew I had done something right.

"Take the line. Grab it in the middle and pull it in and over here."

I did it, and the most astounding fish hung flapping in the air.

It wasn't just that I had somehow caught the fish, it was the fish I'd somehow caught. It was small, not very long at all, it was inflated like a balloon in the middle, and elegantly pointed at the head and tail. And it was beautiful. Not just beautiful like a fish: shimmery, incandescent, sleek. It was beautiful just like a girl.

Mickey said, "It's like, wearing makeup?"

It's true. The fish was that glamorous. She had an electric blue body, rounds of rouge for cheeks, and, arching outrageously over the eyes and down the back, two streaks of shocking yellow, which it wore in a kind of flip, like it was hair. Her eyes were wide and open, rimmed in black, and her *mouth*. Her mouth was almost an insult of irony, a joke of duplicity, because her lips were shaped and sensual, puckered into a full-blown, deep-pink, drop-dead kiss.

The General deftly took it off the hook, placed it on the deck, and we all knelt down, more than admiring it.

From the moment it had made its dramatic entrance onto the boat it was obvious to all of us that we were dealing with something superior. Unlike her predecessors, she did not appear hysterical. She flapped only serenely, primly even, as if she were still swimming, or expected to be soon. If she knew she was going to die, she was far too dignified to let on. Instead she projected a certain noble patience, perhaps with human nature, as if she had been in death traps before, and knew from experience that no man had the heart to go through with it.

"It put up a good fight," The General said. "For such a small fish."

"What is she, Dad?"

"Some kind of an angelfish, I'd guess, shallow water, but I'll have to look her up." And he dashed below to get his fish book and dashed back up again.

"It's too small to eat," Mickey said, doting over my fish, adoring it, trying to cup it in her hands.

"My one fish, and we have to throw it back," I said, nervously looking at The General to make sure.

"You could keep this one and have it mounted," The General said, paging fast through his fish book. "It's legal. Or about." He must have already mentally measured my fish. "It would look awfully good on your dad's library wall."

"But is it big enough to kill?" I asked.

But it was too late, I had already thought of my father. The fact is, I could keep this fish. I could just break the law. I could have it stuffed like The General's fish, and bring it home to my father for what didn't happen on the sailboat that day. Except would my father ever remember the fish he never caught? Would he have any recollection of how I had hoped for him the time we sat in the cockpit together? He'd probably just look it over with great interest like any other present and say, "Ah."

"She's not a yellow angel," The General said, removing his Ray•Bans to study my fish, and then putting them on again to study his fish book. "Too much blue."

He kept looking back and forth from my fish to his fish book. Mickey looked with him, and it was just me and the fish for the moment, and I touched the fish with my hands. A decision had to be made. Time was running out. I had to think fast.

• • •

Too much blue. It could be a fish on the wall, and once on the wall, it would have too much blue for all time. It would be beautiful forever. It would never give birth, raise schools of fish, run the risk of losing them, aging all alone. And people, a higher intelligence, would admire it, its beauty would always explain it. But to throw it back, then no one would know. If you thought of it that way, you'd almost be doing the fish a favor, to keep it and mount it and put it up on the wall.

"Sir? How long can it live out of water?"

"Not long. Take your time."

I tried to think of what everyone I knew would do with such a fish. There were only two choices, keep it or throw it back, but there would be many more choices of why. My father, he would throw it back on philosophical, maybe humanitarian grounds.

The General would keep it for scientific reasons. He was farther along the food chain than the fish was and that fact would assure him of his right to nail it to his wall.

Mother would throw it back on moral grounds, not unmixed with sentimental ones. Plus, like Pontius Pilate, she would not want the blood of this fish on her hands.

Clarine would say, "That's a fine fish, now put it back in the water where it belongs." She would likely go by instinct, and hers was reliably accurate and strong.

So far, no one was wrong.

Then I thought of Mary Parker. She alone could put the fish in context of all things we can know, including philosophy, poetry, science, and myth, and how the fish would fit into that universe. Then I remembered how she'd told me knowledge she could give me, but wisdom I'd have to get on my own. Even Mary Parker couldn't throw the fish back for me.

"What are you *doing*? Do you want it to *die*?"

• • •

My head was splitting from sun and from thinking, so I closed my eyes, and from now on, I didn't think, I just saw. I saw the fish swimming again, uncertainly at first, after the scare here on the boat. I saw her start to swim, uncertainly, then more surely, then surely, then strongly. Maybe she would get by on her looks, maybe on her luck. Maybe her looks were her luck. Maybe some charming fish would come and mate with her someday. Maybe she would be protected, because she was beautiful. But mostly, she would be alone in the water. And that was what I could spare her now. But then I saw further, and even alone, she would still have her swimming. That would be the one thing, through all her life, she could count on. So when I saw her swimming, through all the seas of the world, accumulating her own kind of knowledge, and finally dying of natural causes in a cove not far from home here in Florida, I knew what I had to do. It wasn't philosophy or science or instinct or even wisdom and knowledge that made me decide. If I had to pick any one reason, I couldn't, but however it got there, the answer came through my eyes.

When I finally opened mine, The General had my fish in his hands, and I'll never know for sure, but he was probably on the way to the bin with her. I stood up and commanded, "Now, cut that out, sir."

He looked a little at a loss, a little like a little boy who just got caught, maybe stealing a fish. "What's that?" he asked, at once slightly innocent and slightly ashamed.

I pointed out to the vast ocean, to the whole world, to the entire universe, through all knowledge and all time, to eternity. "She has to go."

So, like a good soldier under strict orders, he took my fish and threw it. She hit the water with a shock of color, recovered herself in a streaming dive, and disappeared beneath the surface.

. . .

While The General went to repack the rods, Mickey and I stood astern, gazing into the spot in the water where we had last seen the fish.

"That was the prettiest fish I've ever seen," Mickey said thoughtfully. "She was unbelievable."

Knowing I was making a huge assertion without any hope of ever backing it up, I said with some confidence, "It wasn't only a fish."

"It wasn't only a fish?" For once, Mickey Knight seemed unsure. She dipped her sunglasses, and looked over the rim out to the water.

Then slowly, like a nice slow wave coming on, Mickey Knight smiled. She seemed to like the idea, that it wasn't only a fish. As if she had been secretly hoping all along that it wasn't only a fish.

"Pure logical thinking can't yield us any knowledge of the empirical world," I said, out of the blue. It was the thing I often said now out of the blue. I wasn't even sure what it meant, but always, when I said it, just for a moment, just for a glimmering moment, it explained things for me.

SEVENTEEN

That fall seemed to come earlier at our house than at anyone else's. I know that seems unlikely, but I spent the ten days at home after the McMansion and before boarding school looking out various windows from various angles to make sure.

The tops of the Knights' trees, off in the distance, were still green as could be. Rey McDowell's backyard oaks, which you could see if you pressed your face sideways against the glass, also still green.

But our foliage was beginning to change. It had drawn a faint outline for itself in orange, which appeared to encase only our yard and our house. Out back, the reflection pool was drained of water, its bottom already covered in fallen leaves. The Little-Boy Statue, so stalwart in summer, looked naked and cold.

The best possible spin on the situation was that we had precocious trees. I told myself it was insignificant. You tend to tell yourself they're just trees.

It was the second last day before the beginning of all-girls boarding school. Clarine had helped me pack, and we even had fun complaining how I was leaving and all, but then she had other things to do, which left me with nothing real left to be done except paint my toenails.

It was the one skill I'd learned for sure in Florida at the McMansion. Mickey Knight had taught me, and she was very good. Very professional. You start by stuffing cotton in between each toe and then you take it from there, and if you do it right, you can make it take several hours.

So I took the things to do it and went to the library, because Dad wasn't there. The library had big curved leaded windows, which gave a nice panoramic view of the back lawn. This way I could paint, and while the polish dried between coats, I could look out and check on the trees.

Outside was ideal for touch football, sunny and cool. My brothers and their friends were out there, and this provided some moderate entertainment in between toes. It was not unlike watching TV while you're painting your toenails, when you didn't really care what was on. So I'd paint a toenail and look up to see who threw the ball, and paint another toenail and look up to see who caught it, and so on, for ten toes and three coats.

Luke threw a pass, which sailed all the way down the yard beyond Matt toward the Little-Boy Statue in the reflection pool. I half expected the statue to turn, reach up, and catch it like he was part of the team. But the ball hit its head, and plopped into the leaves in the pool. Matt and his cute friend jumped on top of each other and fell in after the ball.

I waited to see that Matt's cute friend wasn't injured or anything, and resumed painting toes. I decided after they dried a little, maybe I would go out and throw one spiral and one lateral, and call it that and everything, and then say something casual and professional like, "Hey Luke, go out for a long one." You know, just because I could and I was a girl.

I was really planning to do it, even with the cotton stuck between my toes, but then I thought I'd first call some friends, because that's another option you have while you're drying your nails. Besides, I had to tell someone about the letter Andrew John had brought that day in the mail. It was from my new roommates at boarding school, and it was signed Dotti and Ditto. Twins. They had included a photograph of themselves, sitting at the ends of their beds in the dorm. They had thick, ruffled hair and wore fat, black-rimmed glasses. The most disturbing part of the picture, though, was the third bed, in the middle. It was stripped of its sheets and had an old, ticking-striped mattress. The Twins had drawn an arrow with a dark marker. No question, this meant this was to be my bed, between them.

On the back of the picture, The Twins had noted painstakingly and pointlessly that they had taken the photo themselves, using a time-release device on a camera with a tripod, with 35-millimeter ASA 400 film. All that told me was that they couldn't find anyone who would stick around long enough to take their picture. I will say, however they accomplished it, it did capture their worried look, so expectant and sad.

The letter was not so much an introduction as a long, agonized apology-in-advance. The Twins said they were sorry, but they had a peculiar way of lulling themselves to sleep at night, and although it had driven former roommates to other dorms, even schools, they hoped I'd understand and stay. Since they'd been small children, see, they'd made themselves sleepy by sitting bolt upright in bed, and then hurling their heads backward against their headboards until they were unconscious. Since they both did it, they felt it could be due to some gene.

Anyway, you get a letter like that, and you have to call someone. My only question was who to call. Not Mary Parker. She'd already phoned and said she couldn't come to my going-away party the next night. But she didn't tell me why she couldn't come, and then she said she had to go now and she got off the phone. She did promise to write to me almost every day, though, and she said she'd sent me a going-away present in the mail, which I should get at school. So that made me feel a little better. I could call Mickey Knight. But something told me she wouldn't be too tolerant of The Twins and that letter. Besides, she'd probably hot-wire her father's MG so she could come see the photograph, and I really didn't think it was a good idea for her to see it. So I settled on Jo. She could be very sensitive. She could help me analyze this situation for hours.

So I got up and walked on my heels to Dad's desk and picked up the phone to call Jo. But there was no dial tone. Naturally, I said, "Hello?"

Mother's voice said, "Hello?"

And then a third voice said, "Hello?"

Strange silence. Then the third voice again: "Hello. Thank you for calling the *New York Times*."

Then, Mother's voice, in an urgent whisper, very *Sorry, Wrong Number,* like if she didn't keep it down she would die: "Could you give me the religion department, please?"

"Ma'am?"

Then Mother, like she could now see the shadow of the killer coming up the stairs: "May I have the real estate section, please?"

I quickly pressed the off button and stared at the phone. Had Mother said "religion" or "real estate"? And why was she saying it to the *New York Times*?

I slipped the receiver back onto its cradle. I didn't bother to take the cotton out, I hurriedly left the library and hopped on my heels up the back stairs to The Tower.

It wasn't really the old Tower anymore. For one thing, Cabot had declared that canopy beds were not only juvenile, but sexist.

"How can a bed be sexist?" Matt had ridiculed when that happened.

"You're not that smart, for a pig," Cabot had retorted.

"Stop this kind of talk immediately," Mother had ordered, under the impression they were talking about actual sex.

Anyway, now Cabot's canopy bed was in Lucy's room, and Cabot had a kind of austere-looking single with a flat mattress, which for all I knew was stuffed with hay. A bed a monk would be proud of. Which is how Cabot liked it, because she was an artist.

I guess I didn't really knock, which is what you're supposed to do. But I had never really knocked before. Cabot swung around to scowl at the intrusion from the new hotshot swivel high chair she had, also because she was an artist. "Why are you here?"

"Why is Mother calling the *New York Times?*"

She looked at my toes, and they annoyed her no end, you could tell. I wasn't about to tell her Mickey Knight had taught me. That I even felt indebted to her for it. I just started for the bed. She watched me walk. "What's wrong with your feet?"

"They're still wet."

"Do men paint their toenails?"

"I am not a man."

"That's no excuse."

"Perhaps I am a man. I think I'm one inside."

"I really don't have time for this."

"You don't have time to hear your sister's a man? That is like *no* time."

You wouldn't believe how annoyed she was now. The toenails, plus me being a man and all. But I really wanted to talk to her, before I went away and everything, and I wasn't going to be too picky about the subject matter. I decided to try to keep us talking, even if it was all about me being a man inside. I'd have to filibuster her. "If you notice, I rarely cry. All those years all my friends were crying over boys? They came to me. And when we were little and all went to the doctor? I always took the shot first, to show you guys how not to cry. And now that I have to go away? Do you see tears? Look in my eyes."

She deliberately swiveled back to her drawing board. "News flash. Guys cry."

"Not this guy."

"Good luck with it at the all-girls boarding school."

She wasn't in the best of moods, for sure. I sighed and sat on her torture rack of a bed. Then I told her what I'd overheard from the library phone. "I can't decide if she said 'religion' or 'real estate.'"

"Real estate. She's probably looking for a place in New York for when she dumps Dad."

I hopped right up to go see her face. To see if it was a joke and all. She just swiveled more though. "What was that supposed to mean?"

"Whatever."

I tried to take a look at her drawing, but the minute she saw me doing it, she hid it under her arm. "Whatever?"

"They fight all the time."

"What about?"

"Beats me. They don't do it out loud."

"Then how do they do it?"

"Cold air."

She kind of laughed. But it wasn't a good laugh. She was in a really awful mood. So I had to be careful and not act like it was all just her artistic imagination, working overtime, like when she said Dad "lost" a Buick.

"Do you think Dad had an affair?"

"Yeah, with a bottle of Scotch."

"Really? Have you ever seen him drunk?"

"Not exactly."

Exactly. Everything she'd said, I had already written off to her being a teenager, an artist, and in a really rank mood. One unreliable combination. "So you think Mother said 'real estate,' then?" Personally, I was betting on "religion." But maybe I was just wired to hear it, where Mother was concerned.

"Can't you see I can't talk now?"

I peered over her shoulder to see she was drawing tormented people, like before I'd left for Florida. It was so predictable, it kind of ticked me off.

"Stop looking."

"Great. I'm leaving home, and you won't even talk to me."

She mumbled, "I'll talk to you at your party."

"Gee, thanks."

"Sorry, sis. I've got drawing class."

It softened me up, the way she said "sis," and that she had drawing class. I looked back at the picture, and she didn't dive on top of it this time. There was a woman with a tormented triangle for a head who was sitting in a lawn chair, and a guy in a kind of black-and-white Dalmatian suit, who appeared to be starting up a barbecue, supposedly so he could roast a marshmallow he had on the end of a warrior's spear. So I might have been exaggerating a little when I said, "Gee, I sure wish I was an artist."

Snootily, she peered at my feet. "You can paint your toenails."

I took off, and started hopping around the house looking for Lucy, always a safe bet for a pleasant conversation. Besides, I'd gotten a wild idea about Mother and religion and the *New York Times*. Since Lucy was the only kid who was Catholic left in the family, she'd be the one to interrogate.

I found her in the basement, in the cold, uncomfortable room where Dad had once put all the TVs, thinking that would take care of it. But apparently the rules were now worse than lax. Lucy was in there watching a boxing match.

"Jesus, Lucy."

She jumped and turned around on the couch, her green eyes as big as winter apples. "You scared me!"

"Sorry, but you're watching a boxing match?"

"It's for the title," she apologized. Then she added, "You swore."

"But Mother would crucify you if she knew you were watching a boxing match." She had no fewer than four TVs on, all tuned to the same channel.

Lucy's eyes slid to the side. "Well . . . that's true."

Even though she was watching a boxing match, I couldn't help but notice how pretty she looked. She was wearing a very nice dress, one of those little fall plaid ones, with a white pique collar and a wide black sash. She had gotten all dressed up to sit ringside. "You look really nice," I told her.

"So do you." She was looking at my feet though. She really admired them, you could tell.

She was adorable. She had long, chestnut brown, blunt-cut hair, which today was pulled up in a ponytail poised high on the back of her head. And she had those big green eyes, like Mother's. I hopped into the room, the red-tile floor freezing my feet. "I bet even Dad wouldn't want you watching a boxing match."

She looked around to check the coast was clear, then whispered, "Did you know Matt taught me?"

"To box?"

"Uh-huh. He says I'm good."

"He would know." Matt had won the Golden Gloves before Mother made him stop. I wondered if that's what they were supposedly fighting about now. Matt's boxing. Come to think of it, all they had ever really fought about was fighting. Of course Mother had no idea that Luke, I, and now apparently Lucy, were quite accomplished boxers too. "But isn't Matt a little big to be boxing with you?"

"He's desperate."

I was impressed she knew the word, not to mention when to use it. She was incredibly smart.

"I want to win Golden Gloves."

I didn't want to tell her, you know, she couldn't, she was a girl. You never want to tell a girl that, no matter what she thinks she can do. So instead I just nodded at the four TVs. "Which title is this for?"

"Middleweight. WBA."

"Oh, okay." So I sat down to watch the match with her.

There was plenty of blood flying around. I didn't think it was a great thing for her to be watching, but you can't tell a kid what to watch. They'll just watch more of it. "So nobody has any idea you're watching this, right? You just came down here on your own?"

"Uh, Clarine kind of saw me go by."

"Well sure. Clarine." Clarine would never tell you what not to watch. And she would never tell you not to box. In fact, it was Clarine who had set up the secret house rules. The girls could belt the boys, but all the boys could do was bob and weave. "You're not scared of the basement? You're sitting smack in the middle of the house subconscious, you know. I mean, you're well aware of that, right?"

She nodded. "I'm not afraid of the subconscious. But I have to watch the boxers, to make sure they don't get hurt."

"Oh. Then you're sort of like a referee."

"Sort of."

"I see." I mean, *maybe* it worked. Pure logical thinking and so forth.

• • •

I mean, it was a weird way to watch a boxing match. But I didn't say so. She had her own way of watching. Besides, it made it more interesting, thinking Lucy was some kind of extra, cosmic referee. The volume was too loud, but I let it go, because I didn't want to search for four remotes.

There was a guy in white trunks and a guy in black trunks and the guy in white already had a cut above his eye, even though it was only the third round. His own blood was blinding him, and he was wasting a lot of energy just flailing at air. That kind of cut, though not a serious injury in itself, would wear him down from blindness and he would lose. "See that, Lucy? The eye is the fighter's Achilles' heel."

She nodded. She knew.

"He'll never make it now."

"I think he still will."

"Then is that who you're for?"

"No. I'm for both."

It was pretty interesting, watching with her.

In the middle of the fifth round, I remembered Mother and the *New York Times*. I asked Lucy if there were any particular saint that the Catholics in the household were working on these days.

"SaintJude," she said monosyllabically, watching the guy in white backpedal after taking a mean right to the chin.

"Which one's he again?"

She glanced at me with disbelieving big green eyes. "Saint Jude. He's famous."

"Yeah, but I forget. He's the patron saint of what? Is it lost causes?"

"Um," she said, watching the guy in black land a totally uncharitable left-right combination. "He's the patron saint of hopeless cases."With that, the guy in white went down.

"There's a hopeless case right there."

"I bet he beats the count, though."

He did, and we both breathed easier. "What else is special about Saint Jude?"

The guy in black was body punching like a madman, and it was awful but fascinating to watch, but I had a mission, so I turned Lucy's head gently by the chin. "Luce. This is important."

She asked sweetly, "What else would you like me to tell you then?"

"More about what's in the pamphlet for Saint Jude."

"You lost your *pamphlet?*"

"Uh, yeah. About six years ago."

"Oh my."

She jerked her head toward the TVs, as if slipping a punch. We both watched the guy in black feint left and land a brutal haymaker right, which sent the guy in white straight to queer street, stagger-ing around the ring until the guy in black caught up with him and did it all over again. "I'm sorry, Luce, that guy in white. I mean, talk about glass chins."

Lucy giggled. "He's a palooka."

"He's a bum."

"He's a ham-and-egger."

"He's a chump."

"He's a tomato can."

Well. We sure had done Matt's homework.

The referee broke the clinch, then the guy in white was saved by both the grace of God and the bell. They went to commercial. It was for a blue Buick, believe it or not. We watched it like zom-bies together.

After it, Lucy turned to me. "I thought you didn't like the Catholic Church anymore. I can't tell you about people like Saint Jude if you're only going to make fun of him."

"You mean Saint Dude?"

She scowled. "See?"

"That's *affection*," I assured her. "I like the saints. They didn't do anything. I like God. He didn't do anything. It's the Church I think is . . ."

"Is what?"

"Never mind."

"What?"

"Goofy."

She gasped.

"Look, all I need to know is, when you pray to Saint Jude, does he give you some kind of a sign?"

"A sign? Like, a sign? Like a street?"

"Like a single red rose. Like Saint Theresa. Does Saint Jude do something unusual like that? You know. Send you some special sign to let you know your prayer will be answered?"

"Never heard of *that* before."

Really?

There was a break in the interrogation. I wasn't sure what I was driving at, but I knew I was driving somewhere and I sensed I wasn't that far from home. "Lucy. Say the prayers."

"What prayers?"

"The prayers in the novena to Saint Jude."

"Now? During a boxing match?"

"Well," I glanced guiltily at the four TVs. "I don't see why not. God is everywhere."

She actually looked around for Him. "It just seems . . ."

"What? Sacrilegious?"

"No. Goofy."

"Just. Say the prayers."

"Are you thinking of being holy again?" She started bouncing up and down on the old couch. I thought she was going to break a spring, the way she was doing it. "Please, Zu, please?"

"Well, maybe."

She kept jumping, the way kids do when they're way overstating their case, and they know it, and they're deciding to bounce from now on just to torture you, plus the pure joy of it. "Hey, cool it. You're making me dizzy."

She just jumped higher. "You really are thinking about it, Zu?"

"Kind of."

"Are you telling me that just so I'll say the prayers?"

"Kind of."

She stopped jumping and looked angrily back to the boxing match, flipping me her ponytail.

I knew she knew the goddamn prayers. She never heard anything she didn't remember. She could recite the first paragraph of Dickens's *Tale of Two Cities* when she was three years old. Mother used to have her do it for Andrew John Hague, the poet-mailman. "It was the best of times, it was the worst of times. It was the spring of hope, it was the winter of despair. We had everything before us, we had nothing before us . . ." all in her tiny, singsong voice. And you never wanted to get suckered into playing Concentration with her, where you had to remember what the cards were when only the bicycles showed. She'd beat the pants off you.

So I cleverly issued a challenge. "You don't remember them. That's why you won't say them."

"Oh please."

"Then *please* say them?"

"Well, since you're not a real Catholic, if I say the prayers for you, then maybe you should give me something if I do."

I stared down at her. This somehow reminded me of my whole problem with the Catholic Church. I felt like telling her the Vatican had the richest art collection in the universe, yet worldwide, half the congregation was living below poverty level. But instead I sighed, "What do you want?"

She hesitated. "Point seven million dollars?"

"I'm glad you're not getting greedy about it. Where did you get *that* figure?"

She shrugged. "It's the size of the purse."

"Okay. If that's what you think religion is all about. I'll write you an IOU for point seven million dollars. You can have it when you grow up. I'll be rich by then. Of course, I was planning to do something good with the money, like Jesus said, like feed the hungry or shelter the homeless, but if you want it, I'll give it to you instead, and you can buy a gold-hulled yacht or something."

"No, that's okay." She sighed. "I just couldn't think of anything else."

"Well, that should tell you something right there, Lucy, if all you want in life is point seven million dollars. When I was your age, I wanted better things than that."

"Like what?" She looked pretty interested. Pretty earnest too. Pretty pretty. She was a heartbreaker. "If you tell me one, maybe I'll say the prayers."

I scowled down at her. She was worse than I was. But I couldn't think of a thing I'd wanted. So I lost her again to the boxing match.

The guy in white was uselessly attempting the rope-a-dope, cowering back against the ropes in a defensive shell, letting the other guy pummel him mercilessly, in the hope of tiring him out. I could barely watch it anymore. "They should stop this stupid fight. I'm surprised they let it get this far, I really am."

"I think he'll go the distance."

"The one in white?"

"I believe he will."

"But . . ."

The guy in white was stumbling back across the ring with wide, bloody, crazed eyes, trying to simply avoid the guy in black, who was now working up to a victory dance in the middle of the canvas, where he was presently doing the Ali Shuffle. "Hey, Lucy? Has it occurred to you that this fight is like the world?"

"Uh, yes. I think it did."

"It did occur to you?"

"Yes. Quite a while ago."

That's funny. It had just occurred to me. "You mean that it's like the world, and there's a man in a white hat and a man in a black hat, and only one will prevail? Like it's the struggle of good against evil?"

"Yup."

"Man, Lucy. Are you ever smart."

Her eyelids fluttered. "Well, maybe for my age."

I jumped up off the couch. "I wanted a single red rose. I *really* wanted one of those."

"Really?" she said. "That is better than mine."

"I never got one either. Never got one single red rose."

"Oh." She sighed sadly.

I went over and turned down the volume on each of the sets. "Would you say the prayers for me now?"

"Okay. Would you do that to my toes?"

"Sure. Is that what you want?"

"Yes. Plus one other thing. My own Buick."

"You're only nine years old!"

"But all I really want is to drive myself around. I'll save it, like Grandfather saved the Dream Machine. You have to swear to buy me a Buick. On a Bible or something."

"Fine, I'll buy you a Buick. But you've been watching too many commercials."

"OhHolySaintJudeApostleAndMartyrGreatinVirtueandRich . . ."

"Slow down or no Buick!"

"In miracles. Faithful intercessor of all who invoke your special patronage in time of need. To you I have recourse from the depth of my soul and jumbly . . ."

"Watch the diction."

"*Humbly* beg to help me. In return I promise to make your name known and cause you to be invoked. Publication must be promised. Amen, you owe me a Buick."

"What? What's the last part?"

"A convertible, please."

"The last part of the prayer!"

She shrugged. "Publication must be promised, Amen."

"I knew it!" I started walking back and forth on my heels in front of all the TVs. I knew there was something in there like that. "Lucy, doesn't that sound strange? 'Publication must be promised'? What do you think it means, about the publication?"

"I guess, you know, advertise. Like Daddy does."

"That's right. Advertise. Like in the *New York Times*."

"The newspaper?"

I blinked at her. Don't tell me she reads the *New York Times*. "You think Mother prays mostly to Saint Jude? What's she praying for?"

"Money."

"Money?!"

But her mouth immediately fell open and she immediately covered it with her hand. "Uh-oh, it's a secret."

I hopped over and sat down close to her, very confidential. "That's okay. I won't tell. How do you know this?"

She jumped off the couch and turned up the volume on the TVs. "I can't say any more, it's a secret."

"Come *on*, Lucy."

"I can't. It's a secret. It wouldn't be honest."

"It would be honest. You honestly forgot it was a secret."

But Lucy wasn't saying. I couldn't really blame her. I probably wouldn't say either, if it were a secret. I stared at my toes. If I wasn't going to do a protective coat, it was time to take the cotton out. I was sitting there deciding it, so I missed it when he lowered the boom.

"Oh no!" Lucy cried. "In the last round!"

"Which one? Which one won? The black trunks, right?"

You couldn't see, there was too much confusion in the ring. Trainers and managers and everybody's brother swarming in, yelling and cursing and shoving.

Lucy said sadly, "And he might have gone the distance."

Right. In a billion years. But you don't want to tell a kid that no matter how much she wished it otherwise, the guy in white had no chance, ever, of going the distance. So instead I said, "Of all the words of mice and men . . ."

Lucy finished it up. ". . . The saddest are, what might have been."

That night when I got to my bedroom there was a single red rose from the dining room table centerpiece on my pillow. I knew immediately it was Lucy who had done it. So I went to her room and woke her up. She sat up under Cabot's old canopy, rubbing her eyes. "Is it you, Zu?" she asked sleepily.

"Did you do this?" I whispered, holding the flower up under her nose.

She nodded. "I thought you might still want one, and just felt too funny to ask."

"Thanks a lot, Lucy. That's really nice."

"That's okay."

"But would you do me a favor? Would you take it and hand it back to me?"

"Okay." So she took the rose and handed it back to me. I thought it was really nice how she did it, just instantly did it, without asking a lot of embarrassing questions I wasn't prepared to answer. So I threw my arms around her.

"Zu?" she whispered into my shoulder.

"Yeah?"

"Are you going to paint my toes before you go away to school?"

I took her by the shoulders and told her, "We'll do it tomorrow. We'll do it all day. It takes a really long time."

Boy, did she smile. And if that didn't break your heart right there, she added, "And if it's okay with you, I don't want a Buick."

"I thought you might reconsider."

"I want a Dream Machine."

"But a car like that's not so easy to come by. It might take a while. Can you be patient?"

She giggled.

I kissed her. Then I got up and held my rose up over my head and pranced around with it, like it was the championship belt or something, and we were the guy in white, and against all odds, with no chance, without a prayer, we had gone the distance. I held it overhead, then kissed it and waved it, then paraded it around the room and out the door. I made her laugh.

I took my single red rose to my bathroom for water. I put it in my glass and put it on my vanity table and stared at it for a while. The sad part was, if I had prayed for something before Lucy handed me the single red rose and things like handing single red roses really worked, I probably wouldn't have to go away, and nothing would have to change. Or I could have prayed for poor people, and had the whole world change. That is, of course, if it worked.

I sat up in bed until it was late and everyone was all safe and asleep, even Mother and Dad. Then I got up and sat at my window. As late as this afternoon, I hadn't really expected the dark to come at the end of the day. I guess you never really expect the dark to come at the end of the day. You know it's coming, it's coming and you know it, but you never really expect it, even though it happens everywhere, to everyone, simply all the time.

YOUTH

The cradle rocks above the abyss, I kept thinking as I rocked along in the backseat of a Buick on the way to boarding school.

Naturally I had no way to know it yet, but my clearest memory of boarding school would become this, the two days it would take to get there, the backs of my parents' heads, Dad in his aviator glasses and, riding shotgun, a French silk scarf with an equestrian motif around her hair, his copilot, my mother.

It wasn't much of a memory really, but I hate to say, it won my heart. Though I sat there for two days with arms crossed rejecting it, reluctant to confer the status of instant classic, I knew that's what it was—the culmination of every ride in the back of a blue Buick since I was a baby buffered by brothers and sisters. By the end of the drive it had muscled its way into the sacred place you keep such things, bumping off far better stuff, like French kisses, field hockey games, and swimming pools.

It didn't deserve it. Not even due to longevity. Boarding school itself would last much longer. Though as it would turn out, not all that long.

It was really nothing that was said.

I was doing my best to ensure dead silence through sheer force of bad attitude, and by the time we reached the Ohio border, my parents had stopped the small talk. Mother tried one more time in

Pennsylvania, asking bravely what my new roommate had said in her letter, but blowing it by forgetting there were two of them. I gave her the one-word answer. "DottiandDitto."

"Oh, dear. Of course. The Twins."

If the point of my banishment to boarding school was to remove me from the influence of the likes of Mary Parker, I wished, if we were speaking, I could tell them it was backfiring. The farther I got from Cleveland, the more I thought about her, the books she had assigned me to read and the knowledge she'd tried to impart. I thought to myself, If they only knew I'm sitting here thinking, *The cradle rocks above the abyss.*

It was from a book, but it wasn't on the reading list. Mary Parker told me the story. A man sees a home movie shot before he was born. Sees his own baby carriage on his own front porch. Realizes with dread that he once totally did not exist. Feels about as thrilled about seeing his own carriage as he would his own coffin.

It was death, see, except in reverse. But the worst part: the people laughing and waving in the home movie, his own family, do not seem in the least distressed by his absence.

That's what I was contemplating as we sped through the tunnels of Pennsylvania, staring at the back of my parents' heads, leaving home, the family now reduced to the three essentials, me and them, as if hurling forward to a time when the rest of them would inevitably fade away, and you're back to where you started. Them. The end. Just like the beginning.

And there's nothing to be done about it, you just sit and look out at the other cars, and wonder a little about the people inside, but just for as long as it takes them to pass.

In New Jersey, I felt sorry for them. My cursed magnanimous nature.

But I knew it was treacherous to speak. They might take it as a signal not to suffer anymore for sending me to boarding school. My words would have to be carefully chosen, and well spoken. Finally: "Mom? Dad? The cradle rocks above the abyss and common sense tells us that our existence is but a brief crack of light between two eternities of darkness."

There.

They turned to look at each other. Due to her scarf and his shades, I couldn't judge how much eye rolling was going on. But then Dad winked in the rearview mirror. "Ah, Nabokov," he said. *"Speak Memory."*

Well, you had to give him credit for it. I looked out the window. A swift gray Porsche was passing like a self-possessed ghost on the right.

"There's a great line in there. A funny one."

Yeah, Dad? I'd love to hear it.

He waited for a ten-ton oil transport truck to pass, with the word HAZARD flapping furiously on every wheel flap of every wheel. Then with a grin back in the mirror: "Man as a rule views the prenatal abyss with more calm than the one he is heading for."

Mother looked at him. Maybe we were over her speed limit now.

"Thanks, Dad. I'll remember that at boarding school."

I would be running away from there, for sure.

I mean not immediately or anything, I'd go through the motions for a while, then try not to make a big drama about it—I would probably just pack up a few essentials one night and slip out some fire door. I already knew the most memorable part about it was the drive there, and I wouldn't bother going into it further, if it weren't for Dotti and Ditto, and the strange visits from my parents that fall, and my unusual correspondence with Mary Parker.

. . .

So I'm not going to say how they left me there. I'll just say I had
my personal plans to mourn their absence, and the loss of my
childhood and my brothers and sisters and boyfriend and best
friends and all that, my own plans to see them off at the Buick,
then go cry like a baby about it out by the school pond. The minute
I had seen it when we drove onto that ivy-covered postcard of a
campus, I had it all staked out as a good place to go drown myself
in tears. Forget that I'd claimed to Cabot that I was a guy inside
who didn't cry. But it never happened as I planned, because I'd
forgotten to factor in Dotti and Ditto.

My parents came up to put my things in my room. The Twins
were there, sitting at the ends of their beds, flanking mine with the
bare ticking-striped mattress. All exactly as in the photograph
Andrew John had brought just a few days before in the mail. When
my things were all put away and my parents said to come downstairs and say good-bye now, The Twins thought that meant them
too, and they stood up, smoothed their skirts, and trailed us down
to the Buick. So it wasn't tearful at that point, because of Dotti
and Ditto.

And then, if they didn't follow me right out to the school
pond. I tried to shake them off, I protested they'd get their feet
wet or something, they'd get a chill, but they said they wanted to
show it to me. And the worst part of it was, they were so nice about
it. I mean they looked weird, for sure, with their big ruffled hair
and their thick black glasses, but you've never met two nicer people who just wanted to show you a pond.

"That's the pond," said Dotti.

And Ditto said, "See? We told you. That's the pond."

I'm not saying they were perfect. They were sort of sad and

expectant and worried, just like they photographed. And they weren't brilliant company, nor did their constant presence either side of me instantly endear me to the cooler kids at my new school. They were a social liability I would only grudgingly be forgiven for, and were actually annoying as anything in their own right at night, with their heads bashing ceaselessly against the headboards until they finally conked out.

But really pretty decent once you got past all that. Smart too. You wouldn't think so, with the repeated blows to the head since they were small. I knew all about that from boxers and Matt, but I figured they were one of those famous exceptions to the rule.

What could make you uneasy, though, they truly believed that I was the best thing that had ever happened to them and their room. They really wanted me to be happy there, so there was no small amount of pressure involved. Two people wanting nothing more in the world than your happiness. It was worse than your parents. It drove me crazy, to tell you the truth. It would have been easier if they had been evil twins. But what could you do, they weren't, they were as nice as could be. So I spent a lot of time under the covers with a flashlight, writing long letters to Rey McDowell, Mary Parker, the two Mickeys, my brothers and sisters, even my parents. Besides, it's not as if I could sleep, what with the racket the heads against the headboards made.

My parents didn't write much, they mostly called. The main advantage there was it gave me another way to politely excuse myself from The Twins, because you had to take your calls in the old wooden phone booths down the hall. Rey McDowell wrote love letters, sweet and funny. And he called too, and always said he missed me. And the others also, all proved reliable and worthy and stalwart correspondents.

But Mary Parker didn't call, and she didn't really write either. That is, she kept her promise, she regularly sent me mail, but you couldn't call it writing, or you'd be sadly deluding yourself. What she did was send postcards, that cut-rate blank kind from the post office, with the stamp preprinted on one side. Like Mary Parker thought communicating with me was worth about five cents. Although maybe while I was there, it went up to six. But I doubt it, because I already said, I wasn't there that long.

And then on the other side of those cards, where a person really could write something if they wanted to cram, that side invariably arrived almost blank. In fact, technically, there was more writing on the side with the addresses, if you're trying to prove your point by counting the return.

She sent solitary sentences. Sometimes just phrases. And as phrases go, they were among the most mystifying ever heard.

Her first postcard arrived the first week I was at school. It said: *When creating self, consider.* And that was it.

Then, the next week, she finished the sentence: *...That the limits generate the form.*

This in answer to my twenty-seven-page letter describing every detail of my new school, the old oak tree outside Peabody Hall where we sometimes had English class if it was a sunny day and the teacher was in a good mood, The Twins of course, the dining hall where there was a lot of jockeying for social position under the pretense of just eating a bad meal, even the unusual field hockey uniform knee pads, and my thoughts about turning thirty years old. I'd written an essay about it, in the blank diary Mary Parker had sent me as a going-away present.

"Pure logical thinking" arrived. Which, let's face it, was already suffering from overuse, but she still saw fit to send it three more eye-glazing times.

And here's a memorable one: *Hey, how's your horse?*

All I'm saying is, what kind of genius writes that? It wasn't as if there was a picture of a horse on the other side, and Mary Parker was saying, Here's a horse, and, Hey, how's *your* horse? Or comical, like, Hay, how's your horse? Nor was it even from a fellow horse owner, as in, By the way, my horse is fine, how's yours? This was an otherwise blank card, coming with no frame or reference, out of nowhere, in your mailbox: *Hey, how's your horse?*

I got that and thought, How should I know? He's in Ohio, and he never writes, he never calls. . . . If you think about it, and seriously, how can you not, this postcard was rather scary. I mean, maybe *you* tell *me* how's my horse. Do you know something I don't about my horse? It was like something out of *The Godfather*, which I had seen several times with Mary Parker, of course. Anyway, I got that one at my mailbox, and believe it, I was looking over my shoulder the whole way back down the long Administration Building hall.

"Fear is the opposite of love" arrived next. As relates to what, your guess is as good as mine.

I tried to get control of the situation. In my return letter to Mary Parker, I devised a P.S., cleverly phrased in the form of a question a normal correspondent would feel obliged to at least acknowledge, even if they said they'd have to get back to you later on that. "P.S.: *Hey, how about The Twins?*" I'd written a ten-page letter about them, describing what it was like at night in my room, which I'd referred to rather entertainingly, I thought, as "the ward."

It worked, in a way. Mary Parker wrote back a long one, for her. That is, it still filled just one side of a post office postcard, but she did go into some detail this time. Just not about The Twins— about advertising on the radio. She informed me that there was a term in radio called frequency, not to be confused with the radio signal itself, and this frequency being the marketing theory that the more often, or frequently, a radio ad ran, the more it "saturated the market" and the psyches of the listeners, and therefore the more inclined people were to run out and buy your product. No matter how much they hated hearing your obnoxious ad for the hundredth time.

After that one, I fired off a post office postcard myself: *The Twins, Mary. Not the radio.*

She wrote me right back. The entire text of her correspondence consisted of one words: *SPOTS.*

I have to say, that one was mysterious.

I just couldn't decode it. I spent weeks trying, but I just couldn't figure why a genius would answer a question about two twins with the one word *Spots.* Then, I was in the Dean's Lecture one day. The dean was standing up there in her red suit, with the fake gold buttons and chains she had such a miserable reputation for. She was giving a special, one-time-only lecture about teenage sex, which should have been quite interesting, but she was totally taking the circuitous route, slowly and painstakingly working up to what some girls later called the "money shot." In fact, the dean was single-handedly turning teenage sex into about the most boring subject on earth. Like you didn't want anything to do with it after all. Or at least forget it for once and take a nap.

But the dean would kill you if you did that. You could tell. She had a stiff white face, and hair so highlighted and so pulled back tight you could see shiny bits of pink skull underneath. And her eyes were like a bird's, just not a pleasant one's. A raven's, I kept thinking. If you fell asleep, she'd probably peck your eyes out. So I was trying my best to stay alert, look lively, and I was doing it by making an enormous intellectual effort to figure out the word *Spots.*

And as a result of having the time and trying so hard, I actually did do it. I figured it out. See, when Mary Parker wrote *Spots*, she really was writing about The Twins. She was just doing it indirectly, by writing about the radio. Media ads, I now remembered because my father was in advertising, are called spots. So Mary Parker wasn't ignoring my questions about The Twins. She'd never been ignoring it. She was simply asking in her own special way if I *was buying* them because there were *more* of them. Because I'd been a victim of frequency.

Naturally, I grinned the very second I figured it all out. I even chuckled a little, in awe of Mary Parker. But unfortunately, that was the very moment that the dean was about to deliver the money shot. And I was caught. Grinning. During a lecture about teenage sex.

The dean and I locked eyes, and I immediately wiped the smile off my face. But that didn't stop her. She still stopped the money shot. "Miss Parkman," she said, "you seemed amused by all this."

Everyone looked to see if I was. "No, ma'am," I stammered, "I'm not."

"Stand up," she snapped. "You're being directly addressed."

I shot to my feet. "Excuse me, ma'am."

But her raven's eyes were going mad on me. I couldn't focus back in them, and didn't want to, to tell you the truth. So I looked at the clock on the classroom wall.

The dean came a little closer to closely inspect me, I think. "We've all met Miss Parkman, haven't we? She's a transfer student this year. She's brought us a joke. From Cleveland." As if that were joke enough.

And then she waited. My heart started pounding. I thought she was going to make me do it, make me explain why I'd been smiling, and if I even attempted to explain the infamous Twins in terms of radio frequency, then not only was I the new girl from Cleveland, I was the new girl from Cleveland who was clearly insane. And as further proof, she has no use for teenage sex.

But the dean didn't make me explain. She just stared at me for twelve seconds, according to the clock on the classroom wall. Then she said, Sit down and pay close attention, and I readily said, Yes, ma'am.

But I guess she wanted to make sure that I did it, because she wouldn't stop staring at me. She just wouldn't do it. I started wondering if she even could do it. You know when a bird gets interested, and can't take its eyes off of you. So everybody else started doing it too, because they didn't need to look at the dean, because the only thing the dean was looking at was me. So the entire room was staring at me when she finally delivered the money shot. "And the man takes his penis . . ."

Which I could have lived with. If only she hadn't pronounced it wrong. What she really said was, "And the man takes his penace." Which made it sound like *penance,* the punishment they give you for sinning and confessing it in the Catholic Church. But even if you didn't know that, it was dead-on funny.

It was quiet as anything after she said it the first time, then, when she did it again, forget Cleveland, we had a legitimate joke. Everybody at the lecture knew how incredibly good it was. And everybody at the lecture knew that there was no way I could laugh. Other girls were coughing and choking and nudging me in the back, and here is the dean staring at me hard and cold like a raven each and every time she chirps "The man takes his penace" like that.

But the miraculous thing is, I didn't laugh. I nodded back at the dean like "The man takes his penace" information was the most useful thing I'd heard in my life. I nodded at the end of every sentence, so she'd know I'd absorbed. It took tremendous willpower. I was practically imploding or exploding or something when the lecture was over and the dean finally stopped staring at me, saying "The man take his penace" like that. All because of Mary Parker and the word *Spots,* and, of course, the source, the Spots themselves, who sat either side of me in class, looking worried as anything that I'd get kicked out. But the interesting thing is, I became quite popular after that.

I'm not saying I didn't come to appreciate my postcards from Mary Parker. At first I'd thought, you know, this is not a major effort to communicate on her part. But then I don't know, they came so often, so *frequently,* and they were so interesting in their own little post office postcardy way, and so mysterious, like something that had to be pondered and figured out. Treasured even, like a thought.

I kept them in a stack tied with black satin ribbon. And at night before lights out, I sorted through and made a selection of which ones to contemplate before sleep. One of the postcards even said: *Even in our sleep, pain comes drop by drop upon the heart until comes wisdom, almost against the will of God.* So while The Twins were brushing their hair and getting ready to bump their heads for the night, I went through my postcards.

There was one every night that always fell out of the stack. It was a different weight, which is why I guess it fell out. It had come inserted deep in the diary Mary Parker had given me, the one in which I wrote about turning thirty. The day I found it, I read it, and I put it in the stack. It was just a piece of paper, really, not even as substantial as a post office postcard. So it always ended up slipping out of the stack. As a result, I picked it up and reread it every night. Frequently, you might say. It said, simply, *Avoid restaurant scenes.*

At first I thought it was an odd thing for Mary Parker to write. Avoid restaurant scenes. It just wasn't the kind of thing Mary Parker seemed overly concerned with. Propriety and good manners and such. Don't get me wrong, she was very polite, even if her father hadn't, our school would have made sure of that. But I just didn't think decorum was one of her big talking points. It was more like something your mother would write. Avoid scenes in restaurants. Sure, Mom. No problem. I'm not so fond of food fights myself. It was only much later that I discovered that that wasn't even what Mary Parker was talking about.

First my mother, then my father, paid me surprise visits that fall. And, when you don't have a house to see your parents in anymore, I guess that's where you're destined to end up with them. In restaurants.

Mother's came first.

The dean's humble assistant, that's what he was called, he came and called me out from class. But he didn't say why. Maybe he said so to the teacher, just not to me. So I was worried as anything following the dean's humble assistant down the metal school stairs and then down the long hall to the dean's office. Worried mostly I was going to hear "The man takes his penace" again, and how was I going to handle that. Would I have to laugh?

But when we got to the office, I frowned. Because there was my mother, on the dean's love seat, looking beautiful but wearing black. She had a black suit, and a matching black band in her hair. That could worry you, all that black.

I looked nervously at the dean, who was wearing another rendition of the red suit with the fake gold buttons and chains. "We have a surprise for you, young lady."

"Hello, sweetheart," Mother said, whisking to her feet and coming at me. There was something funny about the way she did it, though. Not funny like she could when she was clowning around. More like funny like phony.

I backed up a step. "You mean you're the surprise?"

Mother stopped. "Yes, dear. Disappointed?"

"No."

We stared at each other for a second, cautious. Then she came on again, tucking the side of my hair behind my ear. "I was in the neighborhood and thought I'd drop by," she said happily, like, What a whim.

It sounded so phony. The dean thought it was highly amusing, though. "Just drop by," and from *Cleveland*. What a riot the dean thought that sidesplitter was. Turns out the dean could have quite a jovial sense of humor, when your rich mum was around, not to mention looking good and rich that day.

Mother started concentrating on re-rearranging the front of my hair. "So how would you like to have dinner with me tonight in the city?"

"And stay overnight?" That meant no twins tonight. No ward. I guess I still hadn't quite adjusted to that.

"Yes and stay overnight." She beamed. She really did seem quite happy to see me. Maybe it didn't seem so phony now. She turned to the dean and promised to drop me back off in the morning.

"Should I pack?" I didn't want to. I didn't want to let her out of my sight, or she might change her mind and drive off in a Buick.

"Not if you don't feel like it, love." She just couldn't resist rearranging my hair. Every time she tucked it back, I rolled my head to the side and tried to shake it out. After a while of doing this, I realized it probably looked as if I had developed a twitch, so then I started doing it on purpose, because I didn't mind having Mother think I had developed a twitch, because I knew the last thing she wanted was a kid with a twitch, in front of the boarding school dean.

"Honey? Why are you jerking around?" She tried looking at the dean for an explanation, but couldn't take her eyes off me. "What is it, love?"

I almost liked her calling me Love and Honey and all those other fairly phony things in front of the dean. It set a good example. Maybe soon the dean would be calling me phony things too. Maybe she'd pronounce my name correctly, and stop sniffing, "Good day, Boise" when we passed in the hall.

Mother watched me twitch, growing mesmerized, you could tell. Then she straightened up and shook it off. Nothing could kill her buzz. "Don't bother packing, dear. I've got things for you at the hotel."

Things for me too? All in all, this was such a fine turn of events, I turned and twitched for the dean. A really big one. She sat on her desk and lit a cigarette. When the smoke came out, it looked like frost.

Outside, Mother said, "Fine, Boyce. Now you can stop moving around." At least she sounded normal. She was pretty ticked off.

"I've developed a twitch because of this school."

"You have not."

"Have too." I jerked.

"You are not the type of child to suddenly develop a twitch."

"B-b-b-ut I-I am not a ch-ch-ch-child." It took me about ten minutes to say it. I wanted her to think I'd developed a stutter because of school too.

In spite of herself, Mother smiled. It took all the fun out of it, so I stopped.

Predictably, a blue Buick was parked there, safely in front of the Administration Building. The convertible one. Her pet car.

The top was down, because it was an unusually warm, if just a little cool, early October afternoon. Once we got rolling, we drove straight down the road toward New York City. The leaves on the trees were all changed. It was an excellent day to drive around with your mother, not knowing exactly what to expect. You would think that would happen more with your friends, or your boyfriend. Personally, I think it happens more with your mother. Simply put, since day one, she holds your life in her hands. It makes it exciting and dangerous, driving around. Fear and love again, I guess.

"It's exhilarating, isn't it, Boyce?" she called, the ends of her silk scarf flying in the breeze.

"Uh-huh!" I answered over the wind and the radio.

She had already checked into a hotel on Fifth Avenue. A man in a white and gold uniform wrenched the Buick keys from her at the door. "No need to be extravagant," she said in the elevator. "We'll share." Then she opened the door to a palatial suite of rooms.

"Wow, this is sure a lot nicer than my room," I said.

"Well, naturally. It's a good hotel."

"I can't believe how much nicer it is."

She glanced at me, annoyed. "I thought the rooms at school were cozy."

"That's because you saw the model."

"The model?" Mother laughed a little while simultaneously slipping out of her pumps. "Oh, Boyce, you can be so amusing. Really. You're just like your father."

"You should spend the night sometime, Mom."

"You mean those twins? With their heads? Where do you come up with this stuff?" Her fingertips flew to her lips. "Heh heh. The way you always end your letters with, 'The horror, the horror.' That's quite hilarious."

"Well, I hope you're all having a good laugh, Mom. That's why I'm here."

"Look, sweetie," she said, while picking up one of those little cards about steak even the best hotels seem compelled to scatter all over your room. "That's for you."

There was a dress box from Saks on one of the beds. "What is it?" I was guessing a dress.

"Open it up and see."

It was a dress. Under the white tissue paper, a black wool dress with rather stunning what's called leg-of-mutton sleeves. I thought it looked silly at first, but when I put it on, it was short, snug, and sexy. And the arms were all gathered up and amazing. I loved it.

"I like it," I said into the three walls of mirror in the dressing room, looking right through them to Thanksgiving Day and Rey McDowell. Maybe he'd unbutton this dress, down the back. Maybe he'd slip his hands under, onto my skin. I looked quickly at Mother to make sure she didn't sense the potential this had.

"You're beautiful," she said, simply enough.

I didn't say anything. I was listening, though. It seemed significant. Not that she'd said it, but that she did it so matter-of-fact and casual and all, as if there were a certain given involved. Maybe that attitude would soon extend to officially dating the boy next door. We appeared to be making progress.

She went to the bed and opened her suitcase. "I think by now you can fit in my shoes."

The dress was so we could go to dinner at her favorite famous restaurant midtown. It was a perfect autumn night, so we walked down Fifth Avenue, then turned a corner and swung into the prettiest restaurant I'd ever seen. The walls were hand-painted murals, like our dining room at home. But unlike our pale, cracking, pastoral scenes, these depicted bright, colorful Basque flower markets. A triumphant arrangement of white orchids stood on a marble pedestal in the middle of the room. We sat on plush red banquettes at a corner table. The waiters immediately began to fuss over us. I looked around. We were the only women unescorted by men. This made me feel proud of us, somehow.

We were both eating the same kind of fish. The same very flat white kind with a pale translucent sauce. There was also white wine, which Mother ordered, which was uncommon, because unlike Dad, she rarely drank anything with alcohol. So there was the pale fish and the white wine, which I already said, and the silver bucket the white wine was in, plus the French waiter with the red hair, who had announced with a smile from the start his name was Christian. And of course the room itself, the sheer color of it, and it all began to seem pretty perfect, like a very good idea to do it, except just as I was beginning to give her complete credit for it, Mother started to cry.

You didn't even know it was happening until you looked up, and then her eyes were glossing over, and then two tears were slipping down and splashing, right into her translucent sauce. "Oh, dear," she said, staring at her fish, "I'm so sorry."

The way she said it, it was like she was apologizing to her fish. That is, she was including him, while apologizing to everyone, everywhere, for everything. I mean, not just for crying, is all.

But I focused in. "Is it *Dad?*"

I thought, you know, Dad did something. Something ugly and awful. Another woman. I narrowed my eyes. "He did something. Didn't he."

"No, dear. Dear no."

At least we both knew what we were talking about. I sat back, relieved. Mother was still crying, but just a little bit, and you probably had to be sitting as close as I was to know it was all going on. "Oh, this is so stupid." She sighed.

"But what's so stupid?"

She dabbed at the corner of an eye with her dinner napkin and repeated the gesture at the corners of her mouth. "Honey, try not to use that word."

Forget it. I wasn't even going to mention it. She was crying.

Mother now laughed the light but tortured laugh that is almost obligatory with public tears. "Forgive me, darling. I can't in good conscience drag you into this. I'm not even angry with him anymore." She put her napkin down. "There. It's over." She leaned and patted my hand. "You're very sweet." And she stood to excuse herself.

I took the opportunity to grab her arm. "Is it divorce?"

The man at the next table looked over, looked her over, and waited to hear it. Mother freed her arm. "Of course not," she said, glancing at the man and then blaming him on me, giving me The Look, then gliding off, completely poised, toward the ladies' room. The man at the next table and I met eyes and both looked quickly at a wall.

Mother didn't come back for so long I thought maybe she was calling home and apologizing to everyone for everything on the phone. You had to wonder if the fight was still on about fighting, if she'd found Lucy boxing in the basement, and couldn't forgive Dad for starting it all by installing the official equipment to do it down there. And you really had to wonder why she'd driven all this way in a Buick alone. She'd said she was on a shopping trip, and to visit her sisters. It was probably true but it still sounded suspicious. Like where were my favorite aunts now? I'd asked, but she'd said, uh, they were out of town. That, plus being alone at the table next to the man who couldn't be trusted to look at his wall, and I started wishing I could go make a phone call myself, maybe to Mary Parker.

I mean definitely to Mary Parker. She had educated me and all, but I didn't know that was going to be it. That I wouldn't be able to keep going back for more. That all the knowledge I'd ever get now you could fit on a post office postcard. A normal best friend you could call up and ask what's wrong with your mother. But if I called Mary Parker, she'd probably just say something like, a rose is a rose is a rose. And leave it for me to decode.

But I'd write her at length about the incident anyway, I knew that. I'd write that before tonight, I had seen my mother cry only once, but that was long ago and it was from actual physical pain. The time she had been standing over Luke when he was little, helping him with a picture puzzle, when he gleefully threw up his spastic baby arms, plunging a piece of puzzle deep into her eye. How we were all awestruck as they came to take her to the hospital. That it hadn't occurred to us that she could be hurt, that she was capable of bleeding and crying like we did when we fell on cement and skinned our knees, or fell off a horse and broke a bone.

But then she'd come home from the hospital wearing dark glasses, looking glamorous as ever, so we quickly and willfully forgot. That it was much better believing she couldn't feel pain. Except then you end up here, not knowing what your mother's crying about. The person you've known longest in your life, and you have no idea what she cries about. You could ask her, I thought. Just ask her what she cries about. But maybe she wouldn't tell you. Or maybe she'd tell you something, but not that. I looked nervously around the restaurant, wondering when she would come back.

From across the room, a young man was staring right at me, while nodding to the older man he was with, who I decided was definitely his father. But since he was nodding in my direction, it was easy to imagine he was listening to me and agreeing with me, that we were having dinner together and not with our parents. He had light, pretty curls that fell to his shoulders, which made him look like an angel, one of those male ones you don't often see. He looked slightly sad like an angel too. How they often hold their wings out, flip side up, in a gesture of resignation, or wisdom that is too profound. Maybe his father was telling him he was getting a divorce from his mother.

Two tables over, a young couple was arguing. Each time one of them spoke, the other one interrupted and said they were making too much noise. I decided they were either arguing about getting married, or had already done that and now had to start all over again and argue about getting divorced.

In fact, as you looked around more, you began to wonder why this was everybody's favorite famous restaurant. Everyone was almost on the verge of tears. I shrugged for the male angel. And he returned it, as if telling me not to worry, it was just something in the sauce.

Mother slid into her seat. Her mouth was redone in red and her usual pretty smile perfectly intact. When I saw it, I knew I probably wouldn't have the nerve to ask.

She touched my hand. "Honey, it's wrong of me to worry you when you're not even home this year. Daddy and I are just having a little difference of opinion." She glanced over at the man and his wall, leaned in and added, "You know what you said before will never happen to your father and me."

But what I did, I leaned in too. "Say you did get a divorce. Then who would get us?" And even as I said it, it wasn't at all what I'd ever intended to ask.

Even so, the last thing I expected was an answer to that question. But Mother picked up her napkin and held it midair. "Well, I suppose that will be up to all of you. You kids can choose." And she happily put the napkin in her lap.

I stared at her. That was *cold*.

"You asked me a question. I gave you an answer." She picked up her fork. "It's an interesting question."

I guess it was, after all.

Christian, the red-haired French waiter, reappeared and poured wine. "Do you even drink?" I said, watching Christian take off.

"Oh, I drink, dear. Every once in a while. Would you like some white wine?"

Sure. I was underage. I'd love some white wine.

Soon Christian swung by and poured my second, then third, glass. Mother's was still full, so he just did a smooth French fake over hers.

So maybe it was the white wine, then, which accounts for the scene that came next. It started making me braver, that is, but just not brave enough. So instead of coming right out and asking Mother what I knew I should ask her, I warmed up by asking her questions a philosopher couldn't answer. I hiccuped first, but she didn't hear it. She was reconnecting with her fish. "Mom?"

"Yes, dear?"

"If a tree falls in the woods and nobody hears it fall, does it make a sound?"

She answered right off. "I've always thought they should put a tape recorder in the woods and settle that."

I said, "That's a *good answer*, Mom!!!"

"Honey, keep your voice down."

Then I asked her, "Do you think pure logical thinking can yield us any knowledge of the empirical world?"

She blinked at that. Then she said, "I suppose not, no." And she went back to her fish.

"Mom?"

"Yes?"

I took a gulp of white wine. "Is it easier for a camel to crawl through the eye of a needle than for a rich man to enter the kingdom of heaven?"

She looked up at me and frowned. "That's in the Bible."

"Yeah, but who ever thought it up?"

"Well, if it's in the Bible, it had to be God."

"Yeah, but what *about* it? Huh?" I shook my head gravely. "It doesn't look good for rich people, does it?"

"Honey, maybe you've had enough wine."

"Here's how you handle it, Mom. In my mind, I make it a very big needle. But you have the option of making a very small camel. Is that how you do it, Mom? Make a very small camel?"

"Now I have no idea what you're talking about."

I leaned in and whispered, "What you have to do is, outsmart the Bible. Just make it a big needle! Or a small camel! Then the rich man can go to heaven!"

She took her own gulp of white wine. "Are these some of the things you're learning in school?"

"No, Mother. I don't learn anything in school."

Then, just like that, I started doing what I'd planned to do all along out by the school pond. I started crying. I mean, not sobbing; I even caught one of the slippery tears in time, but the one on the other side dashed through my fingers.

Mother put down her fork. "Oh, no."

So then do you know what I did? I started laughing. I mean not roaring. Just another hiccup first off, then a chuckle, then a small sob, then ha ha, then a couple more pond-size tears. "Honey, get ahold of yourself. Are you happy or sad?"

I said, "I don't even know, Mom. I'd have to ask Mary," I sobbed, "Parker."

• • •

Christian appeared at the wave of her hand. Mother reached over, picked up my wineglass, and turned it in. Then she stood up, took me by the sleeve, and paced me like a pony to the ladies' room. As she dabbed my face with cold water, it looked as if she didn't know whether to laugh or cry herself. "You may have to run that by me again, about the small camels.

"It's my fault, but you're going to have a headache in the morning."

But I didn't think it was her fault and I'd have a headache in the morning. I thought, in the morning back at school, and then at night between The Twins, I'd be thinking what a night I'd had in New York at dinner with my mother. I guess sometimes you can watch your mother cry for the first half of the meal, and then cry yourself for the second, and still have quite a laugh together.

I giggled.

After we finished the hot, luscious chocolate soufflés Christian deftly served us, and then stood to leave, the male angel smiled at me. Mother saw. "I think that good-looking young man there has eyes for my girl."

Then we went back to the hotel and both crawled into the same bed together and slept, determined to close our eyes, and keep on dreaming.

When Dad arrived at school for his restaurant scene a month later, he didn't do it in a blue Buick but in a black limousine.

He didn't go to the dean's office first; he simply rode up, strode into the bottom of the Administration Building, and stood there like a cowboy in his Sunday clothes, looking from one face to another, stubbornly waiting to claim me.

Dotti and Ditto saw him first. Their lockers were on either side of mine. They pushed their glasses up their noses. "Who *is* that?" they said. They were pretty blind.

I turned to see the tall, handsome man in the business suit, standing in the middle of the noisy hall, searching faces. Nothing looked so utterly alien amid all those swarming girls in uniform as a real man, an actual father. I felt a pang, something thrilling as I realized I knew him. I ran to hug his waist in the middle of the hall.

"Do you have to ask the dean?" I asked after he said he would take me to dinner.

"I did that, from the car."

You knew he would have. He hated even the idea of asking a dean, let alone going, hat in hand, to get permission to take me to dinner. "I'll just go sign out then."

He flipped his topcoat over his shoulder, holding it with the little rope they put in the collar so men can hold it that way. "Good. Dress for dinner. I'll be in the car."

For some reason, I couldn't achieve the same effect with my black dress with the leg-of-mutton sleeves. It looked more like the dress I thought it was when it first came out of the box, a dress for a young girl. I started wondering if my mother had known the dress would self-destruct like this, had seen right through the plans I had for it and Thanksgiving Day and Rey McDowell.

Dotti and Ditto sat on the ends of their beds to watch me get ready. When I was all finished, I held out my arms. "What do you think?"

"It's adorable."

"It's adorable."

Twice as bad as I thought. I dragged the wooden chair so I could stand and see in the mirror. At least it was black.

For jewelry, I wore the pearls my grandfather had given my father to give me for my thirteenth birthday. Fixing the clasp, I remembered what Mother had once said about pearls, that "pearls are a sign of tears." Now I asked Dotti and Ditto, "Did you hear that pearls are a sign of tears?"

They both turned to check with each other. "Who said that?" asked Dotti.

"My mother. But I forgot to ask her what kind of tears, happy or sad."

Ditto said, "So ask your mother."

"Yeah, I know." I looked at them both. "But I was asking you too." I added, "You *two*," just to be amusing and all.

They looked flattered, which was so sad. All night, they'd try to come up with an erudite answer. I felt so bad about it I got right out of there.

Dad was doing paperwork in the back of the car, jiggling a glass of ice and Scotch he'd gotten from the little limo bar. I climbed onto the jump seat to face him, then changed my mind when the car glided forward, and slumped like he did against one of the doors.

"I love limos," I said, stretching my legs.

"I don't," he said, not looking up. "They only look right at weddings and funerals. But I didn't feel up to the drive."

When he said weddings and funerals, it reminded me of Mary Parker and *All stories end in death or marriage*. "All stories end in death or marriage, Dad."

Dad looked up from his writing pad, thought about it, then decided to take his briefcase off the floor and pack his papers in. I opened and closed a cupboard on the little limo bar. "Refreshing change from a Buick, is that what you're thinking?"

"May I have a Scotch?"

"No."

"Mother let me have white wine when she was here."

"Maybe she doesn't know how old you are."

When we got to the restaurant one town over, it was a different scene from the one with Mother. The room had low green lamps and leather club chairs. Nobody appeared about to burst into tears. Most of the men were with men, and while I wouldn't say they looked totally happy, they sure didn't look totally sad. I was the only girl.

The waiter came but didn't smile and announce his name like my favorite waiter Christian had. This one just stood there, very large and most disapproving, looking at me and shaking his head. "Escargots, for the little lady?" He covered his mouth, stifling a yawn.

Dad said, "Wrong. Right?"

This surprised me, that he remembered how I felt about snails. As a child eating out I'd protested it was wrong to eat something as small, not to mention as slow, as a snail.

I said to the waiter, "I'd like something large."

Dad said to the waiter, "She has convictions." He handed his menu in, reached over and took mine. "The young lady will have the sixteen-ounce New York strip steak, very rare. I'll have the same."

The waiter didn't have to write it down, he'd heard it before.

"I'll finish it," I assured my father.

He laughed. "If you do, you do, if you don't, you can take it home in a bag for the dean."

I got it, and grinned. A doggie bag. He'd remembered what I'd written home about the dean. Although he and Mother had phoned to say that calling a dean a dog did not indicate a major improvement in attitude.

Dad said, "Interesting dress."

I held out an arm. "They're called leg-of-mutton sleeves."

"Well, that's a good name for them. It makes you look like a lamb."

I stared down at myself. It was hard to believe it was an inanimate object, this dress. It had deconstructed even further during the ride from school, and was now completely sexless. "Mother bought it." I sighed.

Dad sighed. "Where?"

"In New York City, at Saks Fifth Avenue."

He said, "I see. And how did you come by those pearls?"

I said, "Dad. Grandfather. My thirteenth birthday."

He leaned over and lifted them up off my dress, studied them as if appraising their value, said, "I'd say seven millimeters," and let them drop.

I said, "What? Are you going to sell them?"

He just scowled at that.

Then, while Dad drank his Scotch, I played with the necklace for a while, remembering how I'd written my dead grandfather the letter in which I'd rhapsodized about pearls. How they're both hard and fluid at the same time. How they're rough but smooth, solid yet watery in your hand. And thank you, because really, nothing else on earth from a grain of sand is so astonishing as a pearl.

I hadn't known what we would say to each other during a whole dinner. But Dad seemed in a talkative mood. He asked me a lot of questions about school, and how bad the dean was really, because he said I made her sound pretty bad. Naturally I didn't tell him about her lecture, though it was one of the best examples I had. He asked how were The Twins and said he thought they seemed like interesting girls. I assured him they were. Then he said, sort of gamely, "Uh, Zu. Did your mother discuss finances when she was here?"

"No." She had never, in my life, discussed finances. As a matter of fact, neither had he. Not to mention, Don't mention money.

"Hmmm." He hesitated, fiddled with the ice in his drink. Then lifted the glass, took a mouthful and swallowed hard. "She was supposed to. She was on a mission."

"She said she was on a shopping trip."

"Did she now."

"Yes. And why are you here?"

"Business."

It was believable. He sometimes went to New York on business. But I watched his hand. His fingers were strong, well developed yet graceful, the hands of a piano player. But his knuckles were white and he appeared to have a death grip on his rocks glass. "And where did you stay with your mother?"

"She didn't tell you? At the Pierre."

He rolled his eyes.

"It's a good hotel, Dad."

"It's an expensive hotel."

"Are you still fighting about boxing?"

"What? Boxing?"

"Oh. Then are you getting a divorce?"

"Are those the two options? Whatever put that thought in your head?"

"Well, I know you had a difference of opinion." When he didn't say anything to deny it, I added, "Dad, a house divided against itself cannot stand." That wasn't even Mary Parker's, it was mine.

Dad looked slightly amused. This was a bad sign. He hardly ever told you anything when he was looking slightly amused.

Then out of the blue, for no reason on earth, just a wild stab at thin air, I said, "I know. You're broke."

I had never used the word before in my life. I don't think I had ever even thought it before. But when I said it, my father grinned, as if I'd just hit the jackpot. You could almost see cherries register in a straight line across his eyes. And he was still like that when he said, "I might be, quite soon."

I didn't like the cherries. Cherries eclipsing the beautiful blue centers I loved so well. I frowned at my father, to make him stop grinning. "Is that what Mother was going to tell me?"

"Your mother has put some kind of restraining order on useful information."

I said, "But . . ." But, you know, look at you.

But the waiter came. When he delivered my plate, he winked at Dad, as if planning to make the size of my steak their private joke. I liked Dad again when he didn't wink back.

I watched him cut into his steak, testing the color. It didn't seem quite real, that he could be what was called "broke." What was the definition of that to someone like him? He'd arrived in a limousine. He was wearing a good suit. We were eating thick steaks. "So is that the problem then, Dad?"

Dad said, "No problem." I watched in silence as the blood trickled out from the center of the meat and spilled over the edge of his plate. He didn't even attempt to mop it up. He just dug in, holding a piece on his fork. "Maybe Mother's right. These things are best left to those at the top. I'm here only to take you to dinner and see how you're doing." Then he added, "I miss the young lady of the family." And he chomped on the meat and smiled.

He'd never said anything quite put like that before. It was kind of a rare compliment, so it kind of shut me up for a while. I surveyed my steak. I knew the waiter was watching, circling, lurking sneakily around behind. I whispered to my father, "To save face, you sure have to do stuff around here."

Dad laughed, amused.

The waiter made a point of not noticing how light my plate was when he picked it up. Sixteen ounces lighter, to be precise. He simply yawned, snatched it up, and carried it off.

I said, "I did it."

Dad said, "And he had you pegged for snails."

But the waiter got me back when I ordered the ice cream parfait, or if you prefer, the passive-aggressive parfait. He went to the kitchen and made sure it was the size of a champagne bucket, and wheeled it out on a cart with another guy to guide it and hauled it over to the table with two hands as if the whole thing was just too heavy for him, and slammed it down as if he couldn't have carried it another inch, and good thing he was such a good and manly waiter, because a lesser one would have let it go in a bad little girl's lap. I had no idea what I'd done to deserve this.

As I was sizing up my dessert, my father was ordering yet another Scotch. I thought it was strange when he was suddenly oversaying his words. The words were coming out all right, but a split second after his lips had formed them, like in a foreign movie with a bad dubbing job. And if you watch a movie like that, you can't even listen to what the actors are saying, because you're so caught up thinking how weird it is to watch their lips move. My father was there, he was speaking, but now his sound track was slightly off.

So what I did, I started pretending I was in a movie with my father, but the movie was slightly messed up, because of the bad dubbing job. I thought of the million movies Mary Parker and I had taken the Rapid downtown to see, and tried to remember some of their titles, but the only title I could remember at the moment was of the movie I still hadn't seen no matter how many times it was on TV every Christmas: Jimmy Stewart in *It's a Wonderful Life*. I watched my father's lips, and pretended he was Jimmy Stewart in the movie, and I was this Zuzu character he'd named me after, except we couldn't understand what the other was saying, because the sound track was slightly off.

Later, when he disappeared into the night in the chauffeur-driven car, he left me standing on the porch of Peabody Hall, knowing I could go in and tell The Twins with some confidence that pearls were a sign of the wrong kind of tears.

There was one other scene at school too, just not a restaurant one. I guess you'd call it a Dean Scene. Still to be avoided, though.

It was second semester. I had the Dream Machine, because, over Mother's not so strenuous objections, Dad had promised it as a kind of consolation prize for having to leave home again after Christmas and go back to boarding school. They had it delivered, because no one wanted me driving all that way in such an old car on my own.

It didn't arrive until after I was back at school after break. The humble assistant came to class with a note saying it was there, and where it was parked, and here were the keys and all. That's the kind of note you waste no time passing around. I was blanket pardoned for The Twins after that. In fact, even The Twins themselves enjoyed a surge in popularity due to the Dream Machine. They usually had to sit in back, but they sometimes got a window, and considering they had no chance of getting a ride, ever, to anywhere, until, at the eleventh hour, I came up with everybody's favorite car.

A strange coincidence happened the day the Dream Machine arrived. I got a postcard from Mary Parker. And oddly enough, it said, *Dream Big*. A cliché. And Mary Parker never sent clichés. That is, she had sent *You can't go home again* before Thanksgiving, right as I was packing to go home. But that was just her sense of humor. But *Dream Big,* clearly, was not. Sure, you could shrug and say it certainly went well with getting the Dream Machine, and maybe Mary Parker had decided this one time to send an old but sweet and relevant cliché. Except she didn't know I was getting the Dream Machine. I hadn't seen her at Christmas, and since even before that, my letters had been returned Addressee Unknown.

The last time I saw her was Thanksgiving, when I slipped out of the house at eleven-thirty at night and took the Rapid Transit downtown to meet her halfway, and we stood on the train platform and talked for just a few minutes before we both had to go back in the directions we came.

She was smoking a cigarette when I got off the Rapid and found her, dressed all in black, in the dark.

She sure didn't step conveniently into the light. She stood back and waited until I found her, in black, in the dark. If it hadn't been for the steady little glow at the end of her cigarette, I may never have found her at all. "Happy Thanksgiving," I said when I found her.

"Really?" she said. "Did you have a turkey?" You could tell, maybe she thought a turkey was not a good thing. A bad one, actually, really no excuse for it, especially on Thanksgiving Day.

"Yes," I said uncertainly. "We had a turkey."

She blew some smoke and shook her head and looked up at the stars, which were all out tonight. "I guess we had one too."

"See?"

She kind of shrugged, like maybe she did, then she flicked the cigarette onto the platform and walked over and killed it with her black high-top.

"So when I get back to school, are you going to send me a post-card saying, *Did you have a turkey?* Like, *Hey, How's your horse?*"

She really smiled at that.

"Your postcards, Mary. Boy, are they mysterious. Sometimes it takes me weeks to figure one out." When she didn't say anything to deny it, I added, "Short too."

"Yeah, but frequent."

"Yeah, but *short*."

She looked at me meaningfully. "Brevity is the soul of wit."

Point taken. "I guess I should cut my letters down to thirty pages or less."

"Nah," She said. "Don't ever do that."

We walked up the platform a little, to you know, see up to the stars, because the way they were out tonight, you couldn't not. I traced my finger to find the constellations Matt had taught me, connecting the dots, and she traced some too, but we didn't name them or anything, or say a word about that. Finally she sighed. "Good old Will."

I thought she meant, you know, good old will. Like in your soul. Will like she had taught me. But then she pointed to the sky and added, "He would have something to say about this."

And I realized. She meant good old Will Shakespeare.

I gazed up at the stars. I was a little worried though now, about good old Will, I guess, and things like Brevity is the soul of wit. I knew that one, who didn't, from Shakespeare class. It was catchy, for sure, but not up to Mary Parker's usual oblique standards when she was quoting stuff. And then I remembered her last post-card, *You can't go home again.* Maybe that wasn't intended as such a joke after all.

I looked at her sideways. "Yeah. Shakespeare. He was good."

She snorted a little. She started back up the tracks. "It's all good."

I thought it was another quote at first, just not a very good one. Except she didn't look like it was all good when she turned and looked at me, kind of looked me over and then looked up the tracks. I was still wearing my dress from dinner, and of course from after dinner, with Rey McDowell. I had my ski jacket on over that. She looked it all over, and looked up the tracks. I tried to see in her eyes, but they were brown and it was dark, and, anyway, she wouldn't let me. She just stared at the stars and said, "What are you complaining about? The experiment worked. You'll hammer the details out."

"But I'm not complaining." I shivered. It was Thanksgiving Day. It was cold out. "I just said your postcards are short." Funny, I didn't think to tell her right then and there that I loved them in spite of, maybe because of, that. That I kept them in a stack.

"But I wrote you, first postcard. *The limits generate the form.* That's why they're short."

Oh, I got it. The form. But what limits was she talking about?

Then, out of the blue, for the first time since I'd known her, since we were four, in fact, with a brave little smile, Mary Parker attempted to small talk. "So there's a lake at school?"

"We have a lake. I mean it's not Lake Erie or anything."

She frowned. "You mean you have a pond."

"Okay, it's a pond."

She walked toward the edge of the platform and then stopped and then turned around. "Just. Cherish truth. Pardon error."

"Okay, Mary."

I knew the truth, a lake wasn't a pond, but what error was she talking about? And then I realized, Oh no, she's going, and she's not coming back. "What error?"

"I mean the way to be. The way to go."

She was going, for sure. But I didn't want the truth, I wanted to see the million movies again, ride the Rapid with her, try another experiment, Gandhi or Einstein or whatever she thought. She had given me so much, no less than knowledge, and if a girl looked at it that way, then if she was going—then I was losing the love of my life.

She started looking the other way up the tracks, already looking for a train that would take her back toward downtown. "Where are you going? Mary?"

She smiled, a little impressed, I guess, that I knew. "Busman's holiday. Literally. Dad and I are taking The Dog. The Greyhound Bus. Remember?"

I remembered. That's what she called it, The Dog, because it was The Greyhound and all. I'd always expected a postcard about it. "But where are you going? And when are you coming home?"

But then a train was already coming. First I saw it in her eyes, and then I whirled around and saw its light, far away, just poking through the night. We had to hurry across the overpass if she was going to catch it. There wouldn't be another for an hour.

When we got to the other side and stood there on that platform, we could see the train pausing, making its solitary little stops along the way. I had a surge of affection for it, the stupid Rapid Transit. There was really nothing rapid about it. "When will I see you again?"

It took her a while to say it. "When you grow up, I guess."

She must have seen in my face I would cry.

"Hey, that's not an insult. That's a huge compliment. You're going to do it. I'd stake everything on it." And she added, "For sure."

And then the Rapid arrived.

She was actually on the train, paying her fare, when I thought to ask her. I had to ask her fast, before the conductor closed the door.

"Mary!" And I sort of ran, up the platform, right up to the train, where she had gotten on. She turned to the conductor, to ask him to hold the door. That's the kind of thing that could happen in Cleveland. If you were young and it was important, the conductor would almost always hold the door.

She took a step down again, and I felt silly all of a sudden, as if my question weren't so terribly urgent to stop a train after all. "Never mind."

She looked at me like, uh, last chance, the conductor is holding the door.

So I asked her. "Why *Avoid restaurant scenes?*"

She shook her head. She didn't know. She'd written it herself, and she didn't know.

"The note in the diary you gave me. *Avoid restaurant scenes.* What's it really mean?"

"Uh. Don't ever write a scene that takes place in a restaurant?"

"Oh. But why?"

"Talking heads, no action, no drama, no resolution, no information. Bad news."

And then, did she smile. Maybe the best smile I've seen in my life. "Just a tip," she said. "If you're planning to write it all down."

And with that, she ascended again, and the conductor closed the door. So I don't know if she heard when I suddenly yelled it, screamed it, really, as loud as anything, as loud as I could, after the Rapid, up to the stars, into the night. "Thank you, Mary Parker!!!"

But I already said, the train was already moving, so I don't know that she heard.

And now it was second semester, and all that was left was the scene with the dean. I had my best Mary Parker postcard ever, because I had it all: *Dream Big.* And, of course, I had the Dream Machine.

So when the dean came to the door of the classroom in a new postholiday red suit with the same fake gold buttons and chains, I assumed it was to complain, in person, not even via humble assistant, how I'd broken some law she had recently written regarding the use of or care of or parking of my car.

Of course I probably wouldn't have been prepared for what the dean had to say anyway, so why blame it on the Dream Machine.

After I got up and came out of class to see her, the dean had me trail her a few paces down the hall. Then she abruptly veered around. "Miss Parkman," she said, "what's wrong with your father?"

It was as if she'd been hiding her right hand under her red sleeve but then had whipped it out to suddenly slap my face, making my eyes sting with tears. "Ma'am?"

"He doesn't answer my letters. He doesn't answer my phone calls. And, more important, he's not paying your bills."

I wished I could look at her then. But her bird's eyes were there and I thought I couldn't take it, so I looked at another clock on another wall. The bell rang. Girls streamed out of class, cut a wide berth around us, and walked on down the hall. I watched them go, then thought I better look back at her now. You know, look into her eyes, man to man.

She might have thought it was insolence. It wasn't. It was just hatred, for the way she'd spoken about my father.

"Tell him to get in touch with me, or you won't be able to continue at this school. I'm sorry. There is a thing called tuition." And the dean left me standing there.

And that was all there was to it. You know, Quoth the raven, *Nevermore*.

I walked down the hall, through the door, and sat in the metal stairwell alone. The other girls had all gone on to the next class. It was funny, almost, here I'd thought it was divorce that would truly bother me, but now that I had a moment to sit and think it through, I saw it was probably truly money. Nothing would work without the money. We wouldn't even know who we were. Rich and divorced sounded manageable. We didn't know how to be happy and poor.

That night I took a look at Dotti and Ditto when they were sleeping. I knew I had been lucky to find two nice people like that in one room. I'd write them a letter and explain everything. They were so nice they probably wouldn't tell everybody either. I wished I could kiss them good-bye, but I couldn't take the chance, so I just stood and looked for a while. Besides, it would be almost cruel to wake them, considering what they'd gone through to get to sleep and all.

Then, because I had the Dream Machine, I slipped out the fire door and simply ran away from school.

My idea was, I wouldn't see them. I would just drive home and look at the house, and see what I saw. Just see, you know, how bad the damage possibly was.

ADULTHOOD

It was cold, wintry Cleveland weather when I arrived.

The night of all nights you want to go home. But when I saw the sign in front of the house, I knew I could never go home again.

I decided right off when I saw it not to make a big deal about how all was lost. Mary Parker said a sportswriter once chastised a baseball team devastated about losing a World Series by scolding, "A child has not died." So I decided not to act so tragic about it that it seemed a child had died.

On the other hand, I have to admit I felt rather bad. I just sat there in the Dream Machine and looked at the house for a while.

That so much information could be contained in such a discreet little sign. That is, there had always been the discreet little sign, at the end of the driveway under a low lamp, and the only words on it you really noticed were PROTECTED BY. But now those words were effaced by a kind of lopsided bumper sticker, with the new words, SOLD BY.

So I took it philosophically, just thinking about the World Series for a while. Then Socrates also came to mind. Mary Parker said on the morning of his execution for teaching, his captors removed the chains from his ankles so he could walk about freely, as a sort of goodwill gesture, to make up for having to kill him later that afternoon. Socrates had terrible wounds from the shackles, and as he rubbed them, he began to think it was the most interesting thing,

211

because he could not honestly distinguish from the pleasure of rubbing the wounds and the pain. Mary Parker said he was very happy to have made such a discovery on the day he died, and didn't complain that the timing was bad. In fact, he felt so fortunate to find out the truth while he was alive, I guess he blew his last day writing about it. Which I thought was terribly sad.

Anyway, I figured I was having a similar problem as Socrates, sitting there staring at the SOLD BY sign. I had lost my family, not to mention the house and, one had to guess, all the money, and that did give me pain. But I felt strangely exhilarated also. Sort of intensely interested, even thrilled. I hadn't experienced something on this level for quite some time. Never, to be honest with you.

I started counting the blank, darkened windows on the facade.

I started at the bottom left and added across. Four windows to the left of the entrance; I noted in case I ever needed the information that they were tall, grand windows, like large, paned doors. Then four just like it on the right. Two smaller windows apiece on the second story for each large one on the first. That was four times two plus two times eight, and add the big arched window over the entrance where I first saw Luke and Lucy come home from the hospital in Mother's arms, and behind that, the landing where I got caught for loving Rey McDowell, and in fact the whole house made me think of my grandfather, who was enriched by it by all of a dollar. But I made up my mind not to think of ancient history and such. The point was, there were twenty-five windows in all, on the facade.

On the practical side, I decided what I should do is drive back to the Oasis Motel on the Ohio border where I'd spent the night before, and take a ride with the motorcycle guy who hung out in the coffee shop there. He'd come up when I was checking in, as the check-in counter and the coffee shop counter were one and the same. He wasn't at all shy about it; he smiled and said I could just call him "Jet." At first I thought he said "Jeff," and that wasn't so interesting. But then it turned out to be "Jet." He was quite good-looking in his black tee shirt and leather jacket. He offered me a ride on his Harley, assuring me that it was a very fast bike, and we would ride at full speed under "a blanket of stars." I found that interesting as well and though I didn't take him up on it then, now I saw no reason not to do so, and maybe after, we would have sex.

Then Jet would hang out in the coffee shop at the Oasis Motel and I'd become a waitress there. I would probably have to support him, but I didn't mind. I know, it was an odd thing to think of when you've just been summarily orphaned like I had, that you'd like to reconsider the ride with a motorcycle guy who hangs out in the coffee shop at a border motel. But I did truly like the "blanket of stars." I would have to write Rey McDowell a letter and explain how it wouldn't be right to see him again. Rey just seemed like a rich kid now. It's not nice to dismiss people because they are rich or poor, I'm sure, but that's one of the very first things I started doing when I saw the SOLD BY sign. You know, separating the men from the boys.

I also decided if I ever ran into my parents in the future, say at a shopping mall near the Oasis or something, I wouldn't believe them if they said they'd been planning to come by boarding school in a Buick and tell me how they'd sold the house and taken everybody else and moved away. I promised myself I'd *act* as if I believed them, I'd nod my head as if I completely understood, I'd say no problem, all is forgiven, but I would never believe them in my heart, never.

And if they asked me out to dinner, I'd accept, but when the check came, I'd pay for it myself with my Platinum American Express card. Then maybe I'd ask them for coffee at the Oasis Motel. But maybe not.

So that was the philosophical part of my reaction to the SOLD BY sign. Kind of a dull reaction, really, except for the sex part of it. It was as if I'd known this was going to happen, it was almost old news, even though I still found the situation intensely fresh and interesting. I didn't start crying, I hardly ever do except in the million movies, and that day fishing in Florida, and all the other times. Anyway, I simply sat there thinking of baseball and Socrates and sex for the longest time.

Were the shutters shiny black before, I felt like asking, except then I realized, there was no one to ask. Cabot, she would know, she kept track of such things, but I hadn't a clue where she could be found. There was simply no way to find out if maybe the shutters hadn't once been green. I could have consulted the Dream Machine, it had been a witness to our entire lives, to every paint job, renovation and minor repair, but I really didn't feel like asking a car. I suppose I was self-conscious about going crazy, like before when I tried to warn all the cars in the garage that the barn was burning and get out of there.

I started counting windows on other people's houses. I had never sat down and taken the time to do it, and now I almost wished I had. Also, it was easier than doing our house, because the others had lights on inside.

It was really quite a neighborhood, when you looked at it all lit up like that. Clarine once told me Shaker Heights wasn't even a neighborhood, it was a realm. I'm not sure she meant it as a compliment though. She grumbled something on another occasion about wall-to-wall palaces. She also said, and more than once, that small houses, especially shacks, had true character. So I sat there trying to see it, the comparative lack of character and all, and work up some timely contempt for the place, but all I could see was that it did resemble a realm, very pretty actually, sort of a fairyland in a way, with the lamps lighting assorted driveways and the lovely green manicured hedges, in which you could sometimes see fantastic shapes like animals if you were in that kind of mood.

So my attempt to look at the bright side utterly failed. I guess I just couldn't get philosophical about it at the moment. In fact, the philosophical part of my reaction was essentially over. A child has not died, and I was getting the feeling to get out of there soon. I knew I should wait to see if anybody came, I looked around for more windows to count, but suddenly I didn't feel like hanging around anymore. I forgot to even glance back at the house for a brain picture when I turned the key in the ignition and took off.

I guess I could call it the ride of my life.

It may have resembled the same old ride, the one taken with Mother on many former Holy Days of Obligation, the traditional after-church tour, except now I was doing the driving, and I wasn't doing it in a Buick. The Dream Machine and I started ricocheting around the old neighborhood like a light beam taking a few final turns on its way to the Milky Way, and beyond.

First we flew toward Rey McDowell's house, and slowed up to sixty just long enough to pass. For one brief moment only, I indulged in an image inside. It was Rey, home from basketball practice, sitting at the kitchen counter, keeping his sweet old former nanny company while she reheated what was left of the dinner his parents had already had. A bead of sweat was dripping right off the end of his old nanny's nose. I felt a pang then for Rey, more because he loved his old nanny than because he loved me, but I made up my mind that that would have to be the end of that.

We sped by the next house down. I couldn't see over the towering flat-topped hedge, but I knew which light in which upstairs window was on. Mickey Knight would be at her vanity table, transforming herself for a future date. Maybe not tonight, but someday, with Rey McDowell. She would win him sooner or later. Maybe they would marry each other, I thought, but probably not. It was hard to imagine Mickey Knight as the girl next door, or even Rey as the boy. In any case, I wished them both luck, and pounced on the gas.

Up the road, on the right, we sped by the other Mickey's house, the impressive old Tudor with the Monet painting on the master bedroom wall. Poor Jo. Her natural-born beauty had proved too much of a position for her to defend. One by one, Mickey Knight had picked off her boyfriends, and then moved on to best her in every course and every sport at school. I felt sorry I wouldn't be there for the rest of her life to run interference for her, she'd never survive Mickey Knight now. But my remorse vanished almost as soon as we passed.

We hung a right and a right, and raced over toward the Academy. I couldn't go by the place without remembering Mary Parker as a preschooler, enacting her early experiments in irony. But there were others too, teachers and coaches and friends. I thought of the smooth-skinned English instructor whose cheeks flushed a deep red, rose color when she taught the Shakespeare class. She believed in me, wanted the best for me, I tried hard to please her, and then she was dismissed for an indiscretion that was never disclosed. But we all knew the parameters: she'd fallen deeply, hopelessly, and illicitly in love. Passing the Administration Building, I could still see the pallor on her face the last day now.

I swung a left in the Dream Machine, careened down the hill toward the playing fields, stopped the car and jumped out and ran up the path.

As far as you could see there was green. No matter what happened to other grass in the Midwest in winter, it was always green here. Splendid, spent, sunlit days flashed before my eyes. Night transformed to afternoon and the stadium benches are suddenly filled with parents and fans. The field is covered with breathless girls in navy blue shorts. The Greek girl, Sappho, she gets hit hard in the ankle with an opponent's stick and you can hear the crack over the crowd. I stop running to watch her make a neat flip in the air, a position she will miraculously maintain forever in my mind.

While she flies, I have a premonition about what courage is, and I'm right, because after Sappho lands, she scrambles to her feet and runs down the field and makes the goal. Later the doctor said she had broken her ankle during the fall.

I knew even then there was a lesson in that. Sappho was the most gifted athlete on the team and Mary Parker the smartest girl in the school. I knew these were the reasons they were there, allowed to come without the money to pay the tuition, but I was betting the mystery ran deeper. Mary Parker said a writer said, "I've been rich and I've been poor and rich is better." But writers are so often wrong.

Though I wanted to run at full speed down the field like I used to, instead I made myself hold my ground. It took all my might not to do it, but I was trying to learn something here. So I watch Sappho over and over, breaking her ankle and jumping up to make the goal, convinced that if I tried harder, threw everything into it, for one clear moment, I would know what matters most. But she was beyond me, just inches out of reach, so I had to settle for building a frame around her, thinking of her for all it was worth, and snapping the picture. Then I ran back down the hill, knowing that at least I had something to take away for all time.

When I turned at the bottom of the hill and looked back up at the green, I couldn't be sorry that once we were rich. I would never apologize, say it was wrong. Without money, I would never have known the genius who created my self, or the great athlete who made the goal. I wouldn't have been admitted without the money, they don't let you in on your looks. If it took money to get me in there, then I was glad. As I got in the car and drove away, I only wished all poor kids had been rich kids too. Everyone deserved one free run on a green playing field.

I don't know at what point it came to me, it was all mixed up by now, one road was quickly leading to another, and the path I took seemed laid out long ago, and I couldn't really distinguish destination from point of departure anymore.

The Dream Machine and I were heading in the exact opposite direction, out toward the interstate and the Oasis Motel—when I suddenly remembered what I'd forgotten since I was ten years old. What I'd relentlessly and religiously forgotten to ask my father. Never once had thought to ask it even though the memory was no less than profound. So I had to stop the car and turn around.

We took the route Dad had taken Easter when I was still ten, first down Euclid Avenue, past the Cleveland Museum and *The Thinker*, still sitting there, leg crossed and chin in hand, still with half a face, one leg, and some arm. But still thinking, and still bombed. They sure hadn't scrambled to fix him up. Seeing him again, all wrecked, all ruined, but still strangely not less art but more so, I started thinking of Cleveland as some kind of philosophical kind of town.

Somehow I knew just where to take every turn. Could be your deepest, most affecting memories have an awesome accuracy, are working for you overtime, and when the moment of truth comes, won't let you down. Quick jogs right and left, deeper back into downtown Cleveland, through a mind-boggling maze of dingy streets, a route as complex but determined to get there as a thought process.

Which miraculously arrived at the clearest vision I'd ever had. The three freshly painted white houses huddled together like hope. *Still* freshly painted, still standing, still looking like a little moment of peace in a war zone. Dad had never sold them to the developer after all. You knew because there was a highway there now, but it had a bend in it, an upward bend, an arc, made from massive girders of steel. And it rose right over the three white houses.

It's a wondrous thing when you're sitting right under it, to see a whole highway can bend. Dad must have made them bend it, but when you're sitting right under it, it gives the illusion of looking less like Dad and more like an act of God.

I stared out at those three white houses and had the wild idea my family was now living inside. But you somehow knew those old people in there hadn't died. They'd had a little help, and they'd survived. I even opened the door to the Dream Machine to go do it, go look in the windows, but when that didn't seem quite right I closed it again and drove off.

We were all set, heading for the highway that would lead out of town and back to the Ohio border. But then I saw the big sign on stilts, and thought I should see Fred's Fish Market one last time.

The Dream Machine rumbled out the wooden dock to the end, and I parked and got out and went straight to my dock post and leaned out over the water, just as Mary Parker and I had done countless times during our truancy on our way to the million movies downtown.

Though I had never admitted it to Mary Parker, what I often did during the silence between us here was flip through the brain pictures Dad taught me to take when I claimed I didn't know what conscience was the Easter I was ten years old. My best one, the one I saved the longest and looked at the most, was snapped not staring at the lake, but right on it, when Dad and I went sailing alone in his beaten-up old boat one time.

It happened when I was hiking. I was hiking off the lee side, which was all wrong, seeing as you're supposed to hike on the high side, the side rising out of the water, to use your body weight to balance the boat. I was so young, I must have thought it didn't matter which side you were on.

So I took it upon myself to go practice my hiking, but I already said, I chose the dead wrong side. In fact, if I kept this up, you wouldn't be able to call it hiking. You'd have to call it suicide.

Dad was at the helm, and the storm that nobody knew was coming was coming, and coming fast. Suddenly all the proportions of wind and sail were off. There was too much of it up, and the jib was so full I couldn't see Dad and he couldn't see me. And it was loud, the halyards and things like that on the boat were clanking riotously against the metal mast. Or I would have heard Dad yelling. Yelling, goddamnit, to get to the other side.

But here I was, leaning out, happily and cluelessly practicing my hiking, and then my back was dragging in the water, then my head, except for my face. The boat was now moving very fast, and I started clutching the guard rail with all my might, and I'm sure I would have been afraid, if, all at once, I didn't see the most promising brain picture ever. It was simply one perfect instant in time. The quickly changing sunlit water, the foreboding sky, the full white sails. A beautiful moment in which all possibility seemed contained, right and wrong, hope and despair, even spring and winter. The best of times and the worst, all held in a certain neutrality, or potentiality, I didn't know how to say it, but I felt certain it would pass. So I took the picture.

And then my head went under. It was only seconds before I couldn't hang on any longer. I was going to have to let go, and drown.

But then somehow that's not what happened. The boat veered abruptly into the wind, and my father dragged me back in.

After that, he didn't care that I was all wet and cold and crying, he sat me down in the cockpit and while the sails luffed loudly and the clanking gizmos made their racket and the wind blew his words out to sea, he knelt down and gave me a long lecture about safety in sailboats, and what that meant in terms of living out one's life in a forthright, honorable, and upstanding manner.

I can't remember anything he said, I don't think I even heard it because of the sails, but I still knew it was some kind of privilege, to have my picture and now to have his words that went with it, like a caption to a photograph. And of course, still to be alive.

But there's a flip side to that picture. I keep it on the other side, which is the good thing about this particular kind of picture, as there's such flexible storage involved.

I took it that same day, after the storm, when Dad rescued two teenage boys who were clinging to the mast of their tiny, swamped boat. That is, Dad rescued the boys, but he couldn't rescue their swamped boat too. Even though those teenagers made it clear the minute Dad dragged them on board that they would rather *die* than lose that tiny blue boat, Dad couldn't do it. Or maybe, he just wouldn't do it. The teenagers started shouting they wanted to go back to their boat, I don't know what they had in mind, all you could really see of it by now was the mast, but Dad told them to put a blanket around them and sit down. Personally, even though I was much younger than they were, I thought those big boys were being crybabies about it. Let's face it, it's the boat or your life, I felt like laying it out for them, You can't have it both ways, You'll get another boat, you won't get another life, You're going to have to choose. Even so, even though I thought all that and didn't say it, I'm saying nevertheless, I was awfully sorry when the boat sank too. I took the picture the moment its blue bow lurched up, just before it slipped beneath the surface.

If the Dream Machine had been young and modern enough to be equipped with cruise control, then one might explain how it made the left turn out of Fred's, opened up on the road, and totally took over the driving from there. I tried to coax it onto the interstate and my plans for the Oasis Motel, but it shied, stubbornly refused the ramp, then galloped like a madman past Cleveland proper, beyond Shaker Heights, through Gates Mills, around the Hunt Club, past the long, tree-lined entrances of the country clubs I had competed against in swimming and tennis, making an elaborate series of turns toward the polo grounds.

It's not what I wanted at all. After the revelations of Cleveland, what could possibly be the point of racing like a quarterhorse toward the polo grounds? Here where we once went to ridiculous parties in tents and sent someone under the canvas to steal illicit champagne. Here where silly women in sensible shoes eagerly replaced divots in the grass, as if believing the notion that that made them part of the team. Here where I first saw Rey McDowell staring at me steadily as an entire string of polo ponies passed. I had no use for this now.

But the Dream Machine seemed to have its own sense of direction and purpose, and even a highly developed instinct for not only left and right, but right and wrong. Because it was the car that decided our destination in the end.

We were cruising down the long road, cutting through the dark park. And it was there, in the deepest dark of that park, that the Dream Machine decided to die.

. . .

I slapped the ivory steering wheel, I ground the key in the ignition, I stomped on the accelerator. But there was nothing I could do to revive it. It had galloped too far and too fast. And now it was dead and gone.

I opened the glove compartment and started digging, shoveling the maps and stolen fast-food napkins to the floor. A tiny flashlight fell out. It was one of those promotional items Dad was always bringing home because he was in advertising, and it had an inscription that read "You Light Up My Life." It doubled as a ballpoint pen. That's how much wattage we were looking at. I scowled at it but still took it and popped the hood and got out of the car.

But the flashlight had a feeble, coquettish beam, with about as much power to illuminate as a firebug. Besides, I couldn't begin to tend to the car, because I had to keep defending us against the terrors of the night. I kept whirling around, trying to locate the exact point of darkness that would materialize, that would have eyes, where the portal would open, leading to the true point of no return.

Maybe I didn't see it, but I sure heard it. The transformational howl. It wasn't a dog. It sounded half-human. It was a werewolf. I ran back into the car, locked the doors, and covered my face with my hands, believing this was my darkest hour. Except one hour led to another, and each got darker than the one before.

I don't know what, if it hadn't been for the Old Trooper.

He just appeared. Floating in the windshield, without any face to speak of, backlit by his own headlights, identifiable only by his rounded brown hat and fringe of white hair. I heard him tapping on the windshield first, and when he tapped again I looked through my hands. It took me a second to see what he was, but I instantly sensed from the soft curve of his hat that he was not to be truly feared.

But I still didn't open the window. He tapped again and I shook my head no.

So he yelled, the way old people do even if they don't have to do it through glass, "Lost your way, there?"

I rolled down the window and blurted, "It's dead."

"Well, let's have a look."

"It's *dead*. Gone."

He scratched his hat. "Are you old enough to drive?"

I showed him my license. He had to get his glasses out to read it and it took him a while to do it, but he studied it very thoroughly. Then he handed it back and looked around at the dark park. "Maybe I should take you home."

He'd chosen the worst possible word.

"I can't go *home*. They sold the *house*. It cost a dollar, but they sold it anyway. And my grandfather died, and now I've killed his car. I went too far."

"Well hold up now, did somebody die?"

I didn't say anything for quite some time. He was patient, even though it was cold out and he kept rocking from foot to foot to keep warm. Maybe he thought I would burst into tears. I suppose my lip was quivering, and my face was doing something strange. But I didn't cry. I finally told him, "A child has not died."

He frowned. "Maybe you should start from scratch."

I mean he kind of asked for it. I hesitated. "Do you want to get in the car?"

"Mine has heat."

So that's what we did, we got in his car. It had a light on top, but he turned it off. And the minute I got in there, I swear, it was like a confessional or something, which also has a light on top. I went on a blue streak talking jag, like the guy who cornered the Wedding Guest on Mary Parker's reading list, the guy who killed the white Albatross and just couldn't get over it no matter what. I mean I told that Old Trooper everything, my entire life story, every single thing I've said up until now, excluding only the restaurant scenes, because you don't make that same mistake twice.

Through the whole thing, the Old Trooper listened politely, even nodding encouragement every once in a while. Once or twice he chuckled, and more than twice he yawned. When I was all finished, he said, "So they sold your house." Which summed it up nicely.

"Yes, sir. They certainly did. I saw the SOLD BY sign."

"Did you call information?"

"No, sir. I don't want information."

He said, "Hmmm."

"I've made up my mind to go live somewhere else. I'd be on my way now. Except the Dream Machine died."

"Now, now. Let's have a look at this remarkable old car of yours."

So we got out again. He had a real flashlight and he poked around under the Dream Machine hood, taking his time, while I stood around thinking what a total exercise in futility it was. I was actually just being polite, letting him look at it, like when you sometimes let someone else try their hand at the lid to a jar, just because they want to so much even though they can't get it open any better than you can.

Anyway, he poked around slowly and played with things interminably and reminisced the whole time; like how he had a fondness for old cars like the Dream here because you can find things on them and fix them up yourself, how Mercury was a good name for a car because Mercury in mythology was the messenger of the gods, how Mercury the little planet in the solar system was a little too close to the sun. . . . All I'm saying is, he really liked to poke around under the hood of a car. While I stood around thinking, "The Dream" is dead, and Dead is dead.

Finally, he put the hood of the Dream Machine down and got in, turned the key in the ignition and got back out again.

He headed straight toward his trooper car with a determined spring in his step. "Cheer up, Zu. You're out of gas."

We drove to the old country filling station, and, very gallantly I guess, the Old Trooper said he'd go inside and leave the deposit on the can. But he came back out with a yellow Post-it stuck to his hand. He opened my door and stuck it on mine. "Maybe you'll check in with the folks before you leave town."

I stared down at the Post-it. It had an address, a street called Seaview, in a town I'd never heard of. I tried to stick the Post-it back on the Old Trooper, but he pulled back his hand.

"It's about twenty miles out, on the lake. We'll fill up the Dream, return the can, and I'll lead in my car, and you can follow behind."

"Oh no, sir. That would be too much trouble."

But he put his hand up. He could be pretty authoritative when he felt like it. "Now sit tight. I have to tell my wife I'll be a little late getting home."

"Oh, sir. Please don't do that."

He held up his hand again and went back in to the phone.

I watched him, through the station window, calling his wife. And after that, after an old man calls his wife, I mean, how do you say no, I won't let you lead me home.

So I decided I'd let him, let him take me to the address on the Post-it. And then I'd thank him for all his trouble and all. And when he left, then I'd just a wait a few minutes until the coast was clear, and be well on my way again.

• • •

He drove very slowly, for a trooper. You know how the elderly drive, their noses pointed way out over the steering wheel. It's the same for old troopers. You wouldn't think it would be, but it was. We averaged about twelve miles an hour. I can't tell you how many times I was tempted to pass. But he was being so nice, I just couldn't do it. He was the perfect stranger, in a way. It's something to strive for, to be a good stranger, a kind of lone ranger, a kind of Old Trooper. You could save somebody's life someday.

I was thinking so fast, but driving so slow, a memory started to form. Memory, I guess its formation is much like that of a cloud. It takes certain atmospheric conditions to form one, like conflicting pressure, low and high, or as I say, driving slow and thinking fast.

The memory was when I once saw Cabot carrying the Bible. I was out by the rose beds when I saw Cabbie walking down the lawn to the reflection pool, lugging a major black book. I knew immediately something was wrong with the picture. The book was too thick for an eight-year-old. I slipped over closer to watch her plop the book down at the edge of the pool, take off her shoes and dangle her feet in the water.

She sat there for a time sunning herself, then she hauled the book onto her lap. She opened it, and looked earnestly up at the Little-Boy Statue that stood naked in the middle of the pool.

"This is the Bible," I heard her say. I mean she was saying it to a *statue*. Then she started reading, to the *statue*, from the *Bible*.

She was telling him about a very long flood. It lasted forty days and forty nights. And Cabot said to the statue, "And the Lord said to Noah . . ."

She looked down and up, and then, I guess so the Little-Boy Statue would be sure to understand, she started paraphrasing for him.

"It says that after God had drowned the earth and everybody in the flood . . ." She looked down at the book, looked up at the statue.

"Except those who went two-by-two into the ark. Uh . . ." Back to the book. Up to the statue.

"That God was so *mad* at himself, that . . . well . . . he'd never do that *again*." She wagged a finger for illustration's sake. "And the proof would be . . ."

She looked down at the Bible and stared for a while. Then she looked up at the Little-Boy Statue and shrugged. "That He set His bow in the clouds."

Huh?

She closed the Bible and put it aside and said to the statue, "So you don't have to worry. You're not going to drown."

And happily splashed her feet in the pool.

It was kind of a critical moment for the casual observer though. I couldn't help glancing up at the clouds in the sky, looking for what God said He put there. But I didn't know what I was looking for. A bow, as in a present, or a bow, as in an arrow.

Then Cabot took the Bible and went back inside.

Memories are like water, one flows into the other, so there were more of them, oceans of them. They would well up and go back, not always reaching the whole way, like incoming waves not always catching dry sand. The problem with this type of memories, though, they flood you up inside. You get so full with them, you almost drown.

Where the 7-Eleven met the McDonald's and intersected with the Kmart and sprawling self-service gas station, is where the Old Trooper took the last turn for the address on the Post-it. And then there was the new neighborhood. The houses all looked exactly alike. All perfectly neat, all lined up on perfectly straight streets, which all met at right angles to form perfect square blocks. Each house had one main window, what's called a "picture window," and each had a small front yard and an attached, two-car garage. If it weren't for the alternating colors, seashell pink, moss green, pale yellow, true blue, it would be impossible to tell one house from another. In fact, apparently my parents now lived in a Post-it.

We swung onto Seaview, which ran along the lake, and was the only street that possessed even the nuance of a curve. That's when the Old Trooper stopped his car and got out and held up his hand for me to sit tight while he came back to mine.

He sure didn't do it fast. But he had a nice, spry way of coming toward me, like a job well done, a mission accomplished, pride in his work that would probably never fade. I felt bad about the trick I was playing on him, I really did, and I got so absorbed regretting it in advance, I forgot to roll my window down.

He tapped on the glass. "You've got about one more block to go. Good luck."

My heart flew up in gratitude. "Thank you, sir." And that's all I could think of to say. "Thank your wife too." I said it again, but it still didn't seem enough, and then the Old Trooper tipped his hat and walked away.

But when he got to his car, he turned around and came all the way back again. Of course, I had already rolled my window all the way down.

"What's that big brother's name again?"

"You mean Matt, sir?"

"Matt. That's it. Congratulate Matt for me on those Golden Gloves, you hear?"

"I will, sir. If I see him, I certainly will."

"Good girl. Just one block to go." He looked me in the eye and patted the roof of the Dream Machine. "Bring it home."

Then he walked back to his car, turned on the light on top like he was open again for confession, and drove off.

• • •

After the Old Trooper left, I just sat there as I had planned to for a while. I mean, it wasn't exactly as I had planned to. Now I felt different about it than I had at the start. I felt pretty bad, to tell you the truth. He'd come all this way like that, and he'd tried so hard to keep me safe, and even his wife, an old trooper herself, waiting and worrying he'd get home okay soon. Plus he'd called me good girl like that. And his cute brown hat, with the white hair sticking out. That nearly killed me.

I mean I knew I still had to go, there was no way I could really live here, but I just couldn't stop thinking about the Old Trooper. I'd never see him again and I kind of hated that. He could only be a memory now, which can sometimes make you wonder if he existed at all. He was an angel or something, maybe a ghost, or maybe you'd just call him Grace, something that just appeared, without your asking for it or deserving it, and boy, I felt bad about going to live at the Oasis Motel. So I figured I owed it to the Old Troopers of the world and anyone like them to at least take a look at the new house and at least, you know, see what color Post-it they chose.

I started the car but didn't turn on the lights. Then I eased the emergency brake and rolled the Dream Machine down Seaview to across the street from 29936. The number was on the mailbox at the end of the driveway. The family unit itself was true blue. The worst, by the way. I turned off the ignition and sank down in the seat.

I thought I should do some sort of stakeout, but frankly, I wasn't in the mood. I knew how to do it, from movies. What you do is what I was doing. Sit in a car and look at the house you are staking out. It's entertaining for about two minutes. It's not even dangerous, as the movies would like you to think. It's not even dangerous if you pretend you're *in* a movie. But I didn't feel like pretending I was in a movie. I was pretty tired. Besides, I'd probably pretend I was in that movie with Jimmy Stewart again, and frankly, I wasn't in the mood.

Then, I don't know why I hadn't thought of it before, but I realized the address on the Post-it was probably wrong. Maybe the Old Trooper got the wrong family, with a name just like ours. Maybe he misspelled the name when he called information. Maybe he forgot and asked for a different name altogether. Maybe they just moved someplace new in Shaker Heights. Maybe they got an even bigger house. Maybe in the great America tradition, they had traded up. I mean who in America traded down?

I knew how I could prove it. The Buicks. So I looked around and got out of the car and walked quickly up the driveway and turned the handles on the true blue's garage. But both doors were locked. The odds were still fifty-fifty. Not bad. I hurried back to the car.

But I still didn't leave just yet. Maybe an hour passed. Some lights in the neighborhood flicked off, but the ones at the true blue stayed on. My eyes started blinking from fatigue, from all the driving since the Ohio border that day and the East Coast the night before, plus the long slow ride behind the Old Trooper, and I thought maybe I'd just sleep a little in the Dream Machine, and then we'd get started for the Oasis for sure.

But just as I was about to take my nap, a white form crossed the picture window at the true blue. I sat up, but too late to tell what it was. Then another went by, and it was definitely a male size, a rather tall male size. I bolted forward just as it disappeared. It could have been *Matt*. But Matt was away at college. So no way it was Matt.

Nothing was happening again, so I started closing my eyes

again. But then a young woman, a girl, a teenager who could be *Cabot,* swept past the picture window, holding something out stiffly in front of her. Not far behind came a flying boy, who could be *Luke*, in hot pursuit. I sat right up straight, holding the steering wheel.

Then the tall male form reappeared in the picture window, walking by with more determination than before. It could have been someone's *father*, intent on settling some trivial family dispute.

Nothing happened in the picture window after that, and I sat there calculating. A teenager, a boy, and a father settling a trivial dispute. That could be any family in the world. I rested my head back on the seat, blinking my eyes, trying to keep them half-open just in case, but not trying too hard.

Then, just as I was giving up, the front door at the true blue opened and a child stepped briefly in the circle of yellow outside light, leaned down, and backed into the dark again. I nearly leapt through the windshield. It could have been a kid like *Lucy*, collecting a shiny white cat. But Lucy didn't have a shiny white cat. Lucy didn't have any cat. We didn't have pets, at least not any that could fit in *that* house. I shook my head, and fell asleep for real.

So it might have been an hour later, it might have been a night later, it might have been a year later, but when I finally woke up, the front door at the true blue was wide open. And I would have known her anywhere. I would have known her underwater, in a crowd, or if she were standing alone in total darkness on the blackest night at the farthest end of the playing field. It was none other than my own mother. She stood there, staring across the street at the Dream Machine, and she would not retreat. And then I saw how they lived here, all of them, in this true blue house out on this great, gray lake, in this place they had no skill or experience living in.

Against every bone in my body and every inclination in my soul, nearly drowning, in fact, I got out of the car, and a current stronger than I was carried me there.

THE FULL
CLEVELAND

"Hey, Egg Man." It wasn't Easter yet but it was Sunday. It was springtime. I guess I just felt like calling him that.

He was standing below, on the rocks. I was twenty feet above, on the bluff. You could tell by the look on his face that it had been a while since he'd heard it.

"Climb down," he said. "But the going's easier over there."

I jumped and leapt and slid my way around the boulders and arrived at a rock not so far above his. "If we manage a few more," he said, "we can walk."

There was no beach to speak of, what there was was narrow and stony. There wasn't real sand. "We'll get our feet wet."

"It's warm out. It's almost seventy."

He got there first. I stood hesitating on a six-foot rock. He extended an arm. "Come on. I'll break your fall."

I wasn't convinced.

"You've got the right shoes. Just do it."

"Just *do* it, Dad? It's ten feet."

"Just do it." And he said it again. And again.

I started to like the sound of it. It could be an ad slogan. In fact, someday it would be. Anyway, I just did it.

Dad said, "There."

. . .

We turned together to look back up at the house. Despite its ordinary architecture and rather cookie-cutter construction, you could consider it a house of character. It had just withstood the punishing wind and cold of a Lake Erie winter. Through its glass front, we had watched, awed by the scope of water and weather. A *Great* Lake, it was known as, and you wouldn't want to argue with that.

But the tough little house had proved up to it. Now it looked almost brave there on the bluff. Even valiant. A bit dumb and true blue, but so essentially American. "You know, it's good. It's like The Little Engine That Could."

"That's not what your mother thinks."

We began to walk up the shoreline but automatically stopped every few yards to turn and reappraise the house. Maybe it was more interesting than most houses because you could never make up your mind about it. The farther we walked, the more imposing it seemed. Its glass front began to appear even lofty, soaring, almost high-minded.

I glanced at him. Some of us gossiped that so was he high-minded, that our new circumstances weren't due to delusional overspending, that he had lost all the money and brought us to live here on purpose. That he was capable of that. So someday we'd know something.

But I told the others I doubted it. I told them Mary Parker once said a writer once said, "Nobody commits suicide on philosophical grounds."

"We have an option to buy."

That sounded like something that happens on Wall Street. Cabot theorized that in a desperate effort to climb out of debt, he had invested heavily, and had taken what's officially known there as "a bath." But we didn't know what really happened. And he wasn't talking. "What's an option again?"

"It means we can keep it for good, for a sum, at the end of the lease. It's affordable." A few paces farther, he added, "But your mother would never be happy here. She'd rather we move to New York."

Ah, I thought. So she'd said real estate after all.

He stopped and picked up a stone. It was burnished and pink, shaped like a cloud. But because it was exceptionally flat and thin, I like to think of it as more like a painting of a cloud. Since we'd moved here, he had given up Scotch and taken up stones. He had a collection he'd found during his walks after work. Over Mother's objections, they were displayed with the volumes of history, philosophy, and fiction on the sagging living room shelves. One thing he hadn't sold with the house were the books.

He tossed the stone from one hand to the other. He was good at catching it too. You could tell: if he got a few more, he could juggle.

"Zu, I never told you at the time because you weren't home, but I'm sorry we lost the house. It was as much yours as mine. Your grandfather gave it to all of us."

I had never thought of it that way. Maybe I didn't mind so much, if it were part mine. I leaned down to pick up a stone of my own, but it wasn't good like a painting of a cloud, so I let it drop.

"And I'm sorry you had to find out how you did. We meant to drive up to school to tell you. But I didn't think it would come to that. I thought I'd be able to, well, keep my head above water."

I remembered how I'd promised myself not to believe these very words when I heard them, but I guess I didn't feel like keeping it now. If it's to yourself, you're allowed.

"We'll get another house. A nice one, if not quite as grand. Next semester, Matt will go back to Amherst, and you'll go back to school too."

I didn't ask which one. I knew he would send me to the Academy for my senior year if he could afford my tuition. I had a tutor so I could make up what I'd missed and graduate with my class. But Cabot would probably have to finish at public school. It still almost astonished us, that important things depended on money.

He handed me the stone like a cloud. "So here's a souvenir."

It was smooth and flat, I liked the feel of it in my hand. I was tempted to skip it. I could get eight, maybe twelve skips out of this shape of stone. I was the current family champion, at least of our first Spring Classic. But I slipped it in my pocket. "Thanks."

"Skip it."

"No, I'll keep it. It looks like a cloud."

"A cloud?" He laughed. "I see."

Maybe he did, maybe he didn't.

We both looked out. Today the water was as flat and gray as a sheet of steel. A huge metal fishing boat stood halfway between here and the horizon, its hydraulic rigging working soundlessly up and down. It was kind of a guy thing to get bowled over by, and as he took a step closer to look, I sat on a rock and watched him watch it.

He was dressed in his same old weekend wardrobe, including paint-splattered khaki pants, canvas shoes, and ripped shirt. He could be any bum on the beach. But he wasn't. He was my father. I had never expected to see him from this perspective, standing on a sandless beach not far from a rented house, but there he was, and it hadn't done much to diminish his stature. I had realized that just yesterday, when I was walking by the picture window. Dad was outside watering the lawn with a garden hose, and a neighbor strolled up to talk to him. The man was wearing a beige leisure suit, white patent leather shoes, and a white patent leather belt. A look known internationally, but especially in Shaker Heights, as "The Full Cleveland." My friends and I used to laugh.

But I knew Dad hadn't even noticed what the man was wearing. To him, he was just out there, lucky to be talking to the neighbor. And, when a few seconds later, I could see they were laughing, I took a step closer to try to hear why.

Clarine arrived beside me at the picture window. I glanced at her sideways. "I bet you're going to tell me those clothes have character." She laughed a lot and slapped at my hair a little and shook her head and walked away. I stood there a moment longer at the picture window, studying the picture of Dad and the neighbor, until I found I was smiling to myself. Not laughing, I mean just smiling. So maybe I already knew something.

I slid back into a cozy spot between two rocks and put my face in the sun, which was just breaking through a new bank of sky.

My father walked up the shoreline. I watched him with my eyes half-open. Maybe I was afraid he'd get into trouble if I didn't watch, the way Lucy watched boxing so the men wouldn't get hurt. But I don't think it was really for him I was watching. Let's face it, it was really for me. It was in my own best interest to watch, because watching him, I inevitably thought of success, and how a father is in a unique position to teach you its meaning. A father is your giant standing at the door to the cave. He can be your clumsiest friend but your fiercest protector. Since so much of what you will become depends on him, he is at once your greatest love and your biggest fear. All I'm saying is, you had to keep an eye on him.

"Hey, you guys!"

I tipped my head back and it was Lucy home from church, high up on the bluff, in the prettiest blue dress with a wide sash tied in a bow at the back. In her arms was Lucy's Cat. Limping behind them was Luke's Dog. These were our first household pets. That's why the names were so lame.

I looked down the beach at my father. He had turned, seen Lucy and her entourage, and was waving.

"We're coming down, okay?"

"Okay."

I sat up to see how she would do it. But she was just standing there, teetering, right on the edge, hanging over the rocks. Under one arm was The Cat. Under the other, now, The Dog. And she was wearing Mary Janes.

I glanced back at my father and realized he wasn't waving hello, he was waving Lucy away from the edge of the bluff.

"Luce. Go get your sneakers. You'll never make it in those shoes."

"That's okay."

"Well, believe me, you better go get your sneakers."

"That's okay. This is easy."

I looked and saw Dad had started back up the beach. Then, suddenly, he was running. Then leaping, like a hurdler, over the rocks, taking one smooth boulder after another. His eyes, steady as anything, were focused only on my sister. It made me glance back up at her, is all. And the look on her face. It was so happy and hopeful.

I scrambled to my feet. "What are you doing?"

"Are you ready?"

Are you kidding. She was going to jump. On rocks like these, she'd break like an egg.

"*Dad!* Stop her!"

But, of course, completely ignoring all common sense, they all took a fearless leap. And landed whole, in Egg Man's arms.